D1259171

Where Soldiers Lie

John Wilson

KEY PORTER BOOKS

Library and Archives Canada Cataloguing in Publication

Wilson, John (John Alexander), 1951-
    Where soldiers lie / John Wilson.

ISBN 1-55263-790-5

    I. Title.

PS8595.I5834W54 2006   jC813'.54   C2006-903133-9

The publisher gratefully acknowledges the support of the Canada Council for the Arts and the Ontario Arts Council for its publishing program. We acknowledge the support of the Government of Ontario through the Ontario Media Development Corporation's Ontario Book Initiative.

We acknowledge the financial support of the Government of Canada through the Book Publishing Industry Development Program (BPIDP) for our publishing activities.

The author wishes to acknowledge the assistance of a grant from the Canada Council for the Arts in the preparation of this book.

Key Porter Books Limited
Six Adelaide Street East, Tenth Floor
Toronto, Ontario
Canada M5C 1H6

www.keyporter.com

Text design and formatting: Marijke Friesen
Illustrations: Malcolm Cullen

Printed and bound in Canada

06 07 08 09 10 5 4 3 2 1

For my parents and the lost world I never knew.

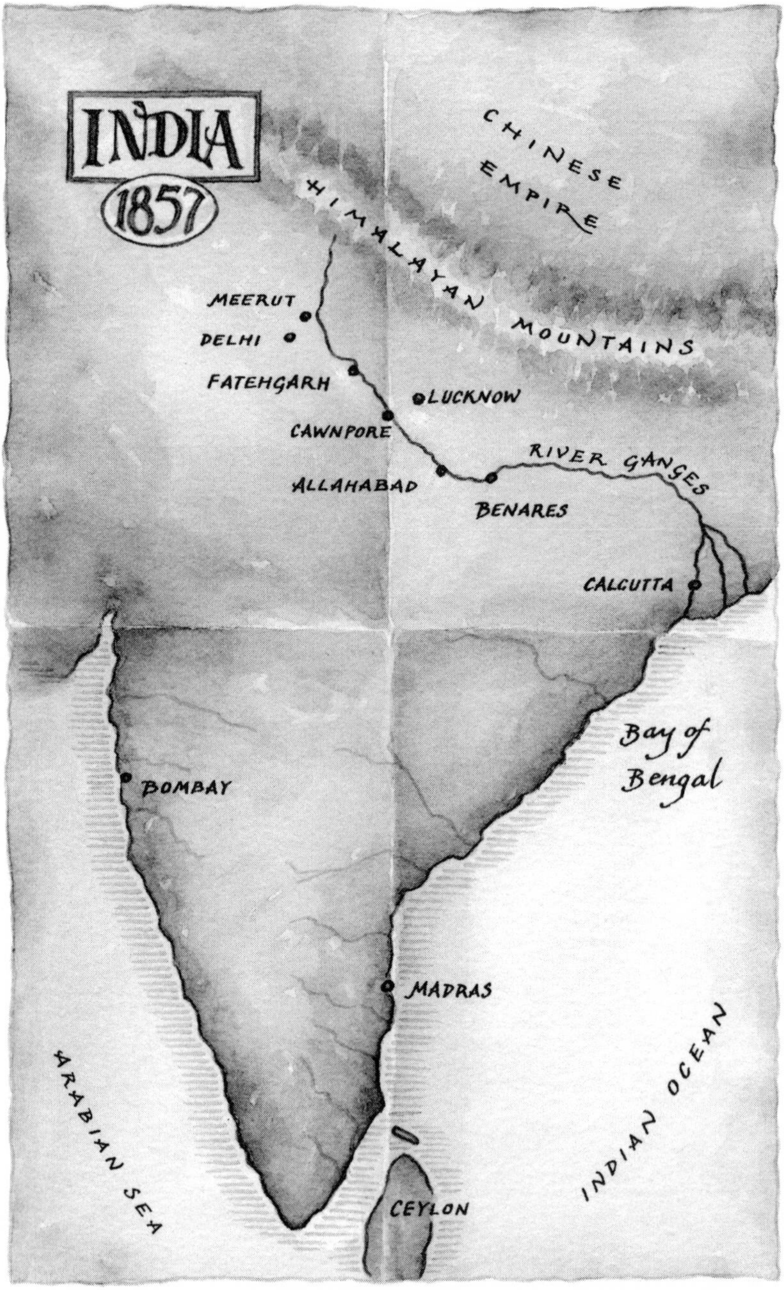
INDIA
1857
CHINESE EMPIRE
HIMALAYAN MOUNTAINS
MEERUT
DELHI
FATEHGARH
LUCKNOW
CAWNPORE
RIVER GANGES
ALLAHABAD
BENARES
CALCUTTA
Bay of Bengal
BOMBAY
MADRAS
ARABIAN SEA
INDIAN OCEAN
CEYLON

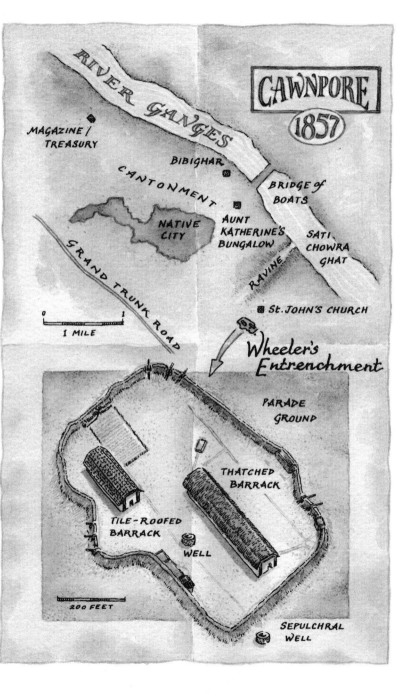

Prologue

Queen Victoria's Jubilee
Sunday, June 27, 1897

The man absent-mindedly scratched the hard knot of scar tissue beneath his left arm where the crocodile had opened his side to the bone forty years before. Was the beast still alive, he wondered? It had been young and inexperienced when it had attacked him and it was said that they could live to be over a hundred years old. He chuckled—it would probably outlive him.

Jack O'Hara was sitting on the stone steps below a small temple, gazing over the Ganges River as it wound across the northern plains of India. When the rains arrived in a week or two, bringing floodwaters from the distant Himalayas, the river would be a two-mile-wide, churning, muddy torrent; but now the water was low, exposing whale backs of sand and mud separated by a weave of sluggish channels.

The river was just as he remembered it: pelicans beat their wings over the water, herding small fish into schools they could scoop into their brightly coloured beak pouches; cranes stood hunched forward like old men in formal waistcoats; metallic kingfishers flashed down on unsuspecting prey; and half-wild village dogs scavenged in the shallows.

Humans, too, went about their business in the river. Laundresses beat clothes on rocks with large swinging motions that sent fine, glistening sprays of water curving upward in the sunlight. Old men brushed their teeth with crushed twigs or ritually bathed, cupping their hands and pouring the holy water over their heads. A mounted British officer—a scarlet wound on the dun-coloured scene—trotted diagonally across a sandbar in the foreground.

The river hadn't changed since that tragic summer when Jack was barely sixteen. Only the city of Cawnpore behind him was different. Now the railway ran alongside the Grand Trunk Road, connecting all the British stations from Calcutta in the east to Peshawar, nestled against India's western border with Afghanistan. Burned-out bungalows, shops and offices had been rebuilt and new army parade grounds laid out with military precision. General Wheeler's pitiful entrenchment had long vanished, replaced by the red brick walls of All Souls Memorial Church. The entrenchment well, where so many brave men had risked their lives for a cool drink of water, and the sepulchral well were both filled in. Quiet gardens and an elaborate monument—overdone and ostentatious, Jack thought—marked the site of the Bibighar and its own well of horrors. In fact, the only well still serving its original purpose was the one in Aunt Katherine's garden. There, a bullock mindlessly plodded the same circular path that its ancestor had generations before.

Jack often thought of his memory as a kind of well. Like a well it provided something good, and Jack treasured his memories of Alice, Tommy and Hari, and of his long-ago childhood in the Canadian forests. But just as the bottom of a well is dark and dangerous, there were places in Jack's memory that were frightening; places where he tried not to fall.

Nevertheless, despite his best efforts, his mind often refused to cooperate. On these occasions, his memories would drag him back to the dreadful events of 1857. Thoughts of the crocodile were carrying him back now, not just to that moment of terror in the frothy, bloodstained water when the beast had ripped his flesh, but to the weeks that had led up to it—weeks of confusion, fear and tragedy. But also weeks of incredible courage and strength. Weeks that had determined the man whom Jack would become.

PART I

The Vultures Gather

Tuesday, May 12, 1857—Dawn

Jack almost fell over the small pile of chapattis sitting incongruously at the top of the verandah steps. At the time he thought little of it, simply that one of the servants had carelessly set down the five round flatbreads—the staple of every Indian meal—while he had undertaken some chore and forgotten about them. It was only later, after all the bloodshed and horror, that their presence took on a darker significance.

Jack stretched luxuriously and took in a deep breath of air, a rich tapestry of fragrances—woodsmoke mingled with jasmine from the garden and cardamom and garam masala from the kitchen. Jack had come to love these scents, but they were warm smells. Sometimes he longed for the cool odour of pine needles or maple syrup.

Although it was already warm, the stifling, heavy heat of midday had not yet descended. It was the perfect time to go riding. As if to confirm Jack's thought, a British officer, resplendent in his red uniform, cantered past, equipment jangling as his horse's hooves thumped on the hard-packed dirt road.

Jack descended the steps and glanced around the large garden. It was enclosed on three sides by a bedraggled hedge of prickly pear cactus and a water-filled moat that was supposed to deter snakes but in which Jack had seen cobras, mambas and the small, deadly krait, happily swimming.

The water in the moat came from the far corner of the garden, beside the row of whitewashed huts that constituted the servants' quarters. A bored bullock plodded in circles around a deep well—a *bowrie*, Jack thought, practising his Hindi—drawing up an endless supply of water skins that were tipped into the ditch by an equally bored old man.

After its attempt to deter the snakes, the water was channelled through a flower garden filled with roses, hyacinths and oleanders and on to the kitchen garden where a few wilted peas and beans struggled against the heat. Finally, what was left of the water trickled in rivulets through the small orchard of banana, guava and mango trees.

As Jack strolled around to the stables, he reached up and plucked a small banana and began peeling it. He would have preferred a mango, but they weren't ripe. Jack loved mangos—the oily sweetness of the soft orange flesh and the way the juice poured out over his chin and hands when he bit into one. Jack's Aunt Katherine did not approve. Mangos were not a proper fruit like firm English apples or pears.

At the stables, behind the house, Australian whinnied in happy recognition. Jack had been in India for a year now and his pony was one of the few bright spots in his new life. Without the morning and evening rides, exploring the sun-baked countryside surrounding Cawnpore both horse and boy would have gone mad.

Australian was named after the famous Derby winner, West Australian, the only horse to win the three classic races, the Derby, St. Leger and the Two Thousand Guineas Stakes, in one season. Not that Australian looked anything like a thoroughbred racehorse. He was a blue roan pony with a dark face and black mane and tail, and a wicked sense of humour. He liked little more than playing tricks on the humans around him, his favourite being to knock Jack's hat into the river whenever they stopped for a drink. Australian had been a gift from Jack's Uncle James—a vain attempt to help Jack settle into this strange world.

Australian *had* helped Jack come to know Cawnpore and its surroundings, but he had never fully settled in. He had little in common with the Europeans in the cantonment. A childhood spent roaming the Canadian wilderness, hunting everything from deer to squirrels and pulling glistening trout from the streams and lakes, had given him an independence and flexibility far beyond his age, and this did not sit well with the unforgiving, formal life his aunt was continually trying to mould him into.

Aunt Katherine, Uncle James and all the other English memsahibs and sahibs were insufferably stuffy and concerned only with appearances. The rigid European society frustrated Jack immensely. He despised the shallow posturing of his aunt and her friends, and the unthinking arrogance of their offspring. He felt more at ease with Australian or the ragged children of his aunt and uncle's servants than in the bungalow's formal dining room, where he had to struggle to remember which fork to use and speak politely to all manner of crushingly boring adults. Sometimes it was hard to remember that India was his country, too. He had been born here sixteen years before.

Jack's Irish father, Major Montgomery O'Hara of the 84th Regiment of Foot, had spent most of his early life in India, leading his soldiers in countless bloody but forgotten battles against Indian princes resisting the spread of the British Empire. Like many lonely officers, he had taken an Indian mistress—*bibis*, they were called. Unlike most, he had fallen in love with and married his. This open declaration of love across such different cultures had alienated the pair from both their families, and Jack's arrival had done nothing to heal the rift.

So Major O'Hara had resigned his commission and retreated halfway around the world to seek his fortune in Canada West. Life had been hard there for Montgomery and his young Indian wife, but they had persevered. Montgomery had not made a fortune but he and Jack's mother had adapted and given Jack a happy childhood.

In the spring of 1856, Jack's parents had contracted smallpox and died, leaving their orphaned son to be shipped back to his only close relatives—his aunt and uncle in the European cantonment at Cawnpore, on the banks of the Ganges River.

A tear stung Jack's eye at the thought of his parents. He missed them horribly, but what disturbed him even more was that they were fading from his memory. He could still picture his father's rugged smile and his mother's careworn frown, but the sharp edges of recollection were becoming dull. He was beginning to have difficulty recapturing the exact tone of his mother's voice as she sang him to sleep with a Hindi nursery rhyme, or the feel of his father's hand on his arm as he steadied the old musket for target practice. Slowly but surely, he was losing them. One day his remembrance of them would be flat, no more special than any of the countless, inconsequential daily events that stuck in his memory for no exceptional reason.

"You will be riding forth, sahib?"

Jack turned to see a small, dark figure standing nearby, his head inclined questioningly.

"Yes, Hari. As I do every morning."

The head bobbed in a strange way that could equally mean yes or no. "Then I shall be preparing Australian."

Hari was the stable boy and the closest thing Jack had to a friend in the household. As far as Jack could tell, Hari was near him in age. He had spent two years at the La Martiniere School in Lucknow learning English and had mastered the language, although he had never managed to lose the singsong cadence that marked his speech or his rather cumbersome, old-fashioned way of saying things. But they could communicate perfectly well. Jack had picked up the rudiments of Hindi from his mother and Hari had taken on the role of polishing Jack's grasp of the language. In the heat of the afternoon when the Europeans sought out shade to lie in, Hari and Jack would sit on the verandah and talk, switching almost effortlessly from English to Hindi and back. Jack told Hari about Canada and Hari explained the complexities of the Hindu caste system.

John Wilson

Jack was fascinated by the multitudes of caste levels and the rigidity with which distinctions were enforced. The four main castes—Brahmins, Kshatriya, Vaisya and Sudra—were easy enough to grasp, but within each there was a bewildering array of subgroups that determined what job a person could do, whom they could touch and whom they could marry. For example, Brahmins, the highest caste, could not eat food prepared by non-Brahmins and if they were touched by a person of lower caste, had to undergo complex rituals of purification. At the bottom of the pile were the untouchables, who had no caste and performed all the most disgusting jobs.

The caste system explained the vast numbers of servants around Aunt Katherine's bungalow—house servants, garden servants, kitchen boys and horse tenders, each with specific duties that could not be changed. Aunt Katherine had a host of maids who dressed and groomed her, and Uncle James even had one servant whose only job, as far as Jack could see, was to shave him each morning.

Despite Hari's explanations, caste was something Jack couldn't understand. He had been brought up to do things for himself and didn't think he would ever get used to the servants drifting around the house like silent ghosts, hovering at his shoulder ready to undertake the slightest task he might wish.

Yet, sometimes Jack wondered if the social restrictions of European society were any better. Sometimes, he dreamed of escape—of wrapping his head in a turban-cloth (*pagri*) donning a loin cloth (*dhoti*) and disappearing into the bazaar. His mother had given him skin dark enough not to attract notice and he could speak more Hindi than his aunt had learned in a lifetime in the country, but the caste system would most likely let him down. Its intricate complexities would rapidly get him into trouble for infringing some custom or rule, unless he went as an untouchable, a person everyone else avoided. The very idea would have shocked his aunt and uncle, but that was one of its attractions.

"Australian is ready, sahib." Hari appeared out of the stable, leading Jack's pony fully kitted out in its tack.

"Thank you, Hari." Jack took the reins and moved round to mount Australian. "Oh, Hari, did you forget some chapattis on the verandah?"

Hari's silence made Jack look around Australian's neck. His friend looked worried.

"What is it?"

"Not good. Very bad."

"What do you mean? They're just chapattis."

"Not just chapattis." Hari walked around Australian's head. "They have meaning."

"What do they mean?"

Hari hesitated for a long moment. "Sahib, they mean trouble."

"What kind of trouble?" Frustration at Hari's enigmatic answers began to show in Jack's voice. "Tell me what they mean."

Hari sighed. "Long ago, before the British came, a Rajah—prince—who desired to know if he could go to war, used chapattis. He was sending them out from his palace to be bitten."

"Bitten?"

"Yes. If a man received chapattis he bit to show loyalty to the Rajah. Then he was making more and sending on. If the man did not want to go to war, he did not bite or send on. When the Rajah heard how far chapattis were going, he knew who would answer his call to war. Much biting was good."

"But that's just a story from the old days. And these chapattis weren't bitten."

"But Nana Sahib at Bithur wishes once more to be Rajah. He is Mahratta, descendant of mighty kings at the time of Akbar the Great. Nana wishes those times to come again. He has, I think, sent out the chapattis."

"But he can't go to war! He lives in a rundown palace and only has a few soldiers for ceremonials to impress the peasants in the surrounding villages."

"Young sahib, these are strange days. Armies can come from many places. Do not touch the chapattis."

"I won't, but I still don't see what harm they can do. Nana has no power any more. Everyone says so."

"You are most correct, sahib. Enjoy your morning ride."

Hari retreated into the stable, leaving Jack to thoughtfully mount Australian and trot out onto the road. The conversation had left Jack feeling strange. Was Hari keeping things from him? Why were the days strange? Jack sighed. Every day here was strange. Mysterious chapattis travelling around the countryside at night! It would be funny if only Hari hadn't looked so worried.

Where Soldiers Lie

Cawnpore was a mess of a city, spread haphazardly along the southwest bank of the Ganges. In reality it was several distinct towns.

Jack lived with his Aunt Katherine and Uncle James in one of the collection of spacious, immaculately kept bungalows in the cantonment. This was where army officers, East India Company employees and European traders lived their sheltered lives. The only dark-skinned faces seen on the cantonment's wide, tree-lined streets were servants or favoured Eurasian employees—or Jack.

The cantonment occupied the best position in town, a long swath perched on the high bank of the river where any cooling breeze off the water could be felt. Behind this oasis of transplanted British civilization loomed the packed and filthy native city. Narrow alleys—clogged with stalls, rickshaws and aimlessly wandering cattle—teemed with life. Shopkeepers bawled the benefits of their produce, scribes scribbled official letters on tiny folding desks, beggars whined at any passing wealth and skinny, near-naked holy men flitted through the mass of humanity like underfed ghosts. The air was filled with noise, dust and the smells of every form of human activity. On his rare visits to these streets, Jack imagined that medieval London might have smelled the same way before toilets and sewers were introduced.

Surrounding the native city were the infantry and artillery lines. For the native infantry and cavalry—*sepoys* and *sowars*—these gave the impression of bustling villages with hordes of half-naked children running between the rows of rough huts where the soldier's families lived. The European lines consisted of low, verandahed barracks set in open expanses of swept parade ground.

On the northwestern edge of town sat the squat, brick treasury and magazine. The city was connected to the northeast bank of the river and the Lucknow road by a bridge of boats.

No physical barriers prevented people moving from one area of town to another, but most were content—for religious, racial and cultural reasons—to stay within their own prescribed world.

Jack and Australian had explored it all, and many of the scattered villages up and down the Grand Trunk Road as well, but their favourite spot was in the open spaces by the river. The air was slightly cooler and cleaner here and there was always activity to watch. The Ganges was both a place to wash bodies and clothes, and the most sacred site in India. The mere touch of its water could cleanse a person's soul of the most terrible crime.

Jack rode down the narrow ravine that cut through the river's high bank near his aunt's bungalow. He emerged at Sati Chowra Ghat, a series of stone steps that allowed access to the river. When the water was high and lapping at the bottom steps, Sati Chowra was often crowded with people washing and praying. But now, in the dry heat of May, the water was far from the bank and the steps were deserted.

Jack turned Australian past the foot of the small Hardeo

Temple to the Hindu god Shiva and splashed his way west through the shallows. At the bridge of boats, he regained the bank. He had intended to skirt the native city and explore the countryside to the west, but the sight of a solitary figure, sitting on a low wall, made him rein in. It was a girl about his age, dressed in immaculately pressed riding clothes. Her long dark hair was held in a tight bun and her left hand lazily held the reins of a piebald pony.

It was unusual enough to see a woman out on her own in this culture that worshipped the idea of womanhood and cherished, pampered and protected any individual considered to be close to the ideal, but two additional things made Jack stop so fast he almost fell out of his saddle. This girl, even seen only in profile, was beautiful, and her skin was nearly as dark as his own.

As Jack recovered his balance, the girl looked at him with two of the deepest, darkest eyes he had ever seen.

"What are you doing here?" Jack blurted out the first thing that crossed his mind.

A gleam of anger flashed into the eyes. "I wasn't aware that this was private property. And what business is it of yours anyway?"

"N ... none," Jack stammered. "It's just ... I mean ... you shouldn't be out alone."

"Should I not?" The glare turned to smile. "And why would that be?"

"It's not ... " Jack searched for the right word, "seemly." Mentally he kicked himself. Stupid! He sounded just like his aunt.

The girl laughed. "And it is your duty, I suppose, to protect lonely damsels from harm and ensure that they do nothing that is not seemly?"

Jack felt his cheeks redden. He didn't like being mocked, and besides, why didn't this girl act the demure way all women were expected to act here? She should be politely thanking him for his concern and waiting for him to offer to escort her back to the cantonment. Instead she was staring challengingly at him with those impenetrable eyes. Jack's brain was turning to mush.

"It's not safe," he said lamely, "or proper." Damn, there was his aunt again.

The smile faded from the girl's eyes. "Let me tell you a story about proper. Do you know what this place is?" she asked, waving her arm to take in the building on the other side of the low wall.

Jack walked Australian forward and examined the scene. The rundown building consisted of two long structures facing a small courtyard that was visible through a pair of wide, wooden doors. The courtyard was empty except for a twisted old tree—a mulsoori tree, Jack guessed. The garden was surrounded by the low wall, but looked untended, the grass long and dry. About forty feet to one side a large banyan tree partially hid the stonework of a well.

"It's the Bibighar," the girl said.

"It's deserted," Jack observed.

"Now it is, but it wasn't always. Long ago it was built by a British officer for his *bibi*—do you know what a *bibi* is?"

"Of course I do. My mother was one."

The girl nodded in acknowledgment. "My grandmother also. So, you know how important *bibis* were in the early days here?"

Jack's confused look encouraged her to continue. "The first British soldiers and traders left their wives and sweethearts at home. They took local wives—*bibis*."

"Like the *voyageurs* did in Canada," Jack interrupted.

"I suppose so. Anyway, the *bibis* taught the newcomers how to do things—how to stay cool in the heat, how to negotiate with local princes—it was a good arrangement but it was doomed. As the Empire grew, more and more men began to bring their wives and families out here to live. As you can imagine, the wives did not take kindly to the *bibis*. These local wives were often abandoned with nothing."

"My father took my mother to Canada West."

"That was a brave solution, but it was not possible for everyone. One young officer built this place for his *bibi*. By all accounts she was very beautiful and he loved her dearly. He built her this house close to the river, with a courtyard and verandahs to catch the breeze. He even built it around her favourite mulsoori tree.

The arrangement suited the pair and, for many years, the officer and his *bibi* were happy. But, eventually, the officer was posted back to England. She begged to go with him, but the young man said no."

"He can't have loved her then," Jack interrupted.

"Oh, but he did. That was why he decided to leave her behind. England is not Canada West. The officer knew that she would not survive either the harsh English climate or the even harsher drawing rooms of proper society. He believed he was doing the best thing.

"On the day the officer was due to leave, he came here to say farewell to his love. He found her hanging from the mulsoori tree. The officer was devastated and, so local legend has it, died of a broken heart on the voyage home."

"That's a terrible story."

"It is." The girl stood up on the low wall and mounted her pony. "Now you see the consequences of doing things the proper way." She pulled her pony's head around and walked back toward the cantonment.

"Wait," Jack shouted. "I don't know your name."

"That's because we haven't been properly introduced," the girl said with a laugh. She flicked her riding crop and her pony broke into a trot.

Jack stared after her until she disappeared behind the Old Cawnpore Hotel. He felt stunned. He had never met anyone like her before. She was nothing like the simpering daughters of the sahibs and memsahibs who giggled inanely and pretended to be utterly helpless whenever a male was near. She had opinions and spoke her mind—and she was beautiful. As beautiful as the *bibi* in her story, Jack wondered? His gaze wandered back to the Bibighar and the mulsoori tree. There was a thicker branch on its left side. That must be where she hanged herself. In Jack's imagination she was still there, her body twisting mournfully in the breeze.

Tuesday, May 12—Tiffin

Jack didn't feel like eating but attendance at tiffin was obligatory in his aunt's house. In India two main meals were taken each day: breakfast early in the morning before it became too hot, and dinner, late in the evening after it had cooled down somewhat. The long gap between was bridged by a light snack—tiffin—usually taken in the early afternoon before everyone collapsed into heat-induced lethargy.

Two servants were employed full-time in attempting to keep the high-ceilinged dining room slightly cooler than the blistering heat outside. One walked around splashing water on the rattan blinds that covered all the windows while the other pulled the rope attached to the *punkah*, a large rectangle of canvas that swung back and forth to create a draft. It was all in vain. Jack was bathed in sweat despite having changed his clothes and washed after his morning ride.

Enough of the razor-sharp midday sunlight filtered in through the blinds to allow Jack to pick at the array of food set out on the broad, rosewood sideboard. He selected a thin slice of meat, a spoonful of leftover fish curry from the night before and a hard-boiled egg.

"Damned nonsense!" Uncle James exclaimed as Jack returned to the table. A folded copy of the *Bengal Harkaru* newspaper lay on the table beside him and he was poking excitedly at it with his fork.

"What is, dear?" Aunt Katherine asked from the opposite end of the table.

"This rubbish about the greased cartridges for the new rifled muskets. Apparently the *sepoys* are still refusing to bite them."

"Why do they have to bite them?" Jack asked.

Uncle James looked up from stabbing his newspaper. Like almost every other European in India, he worked for the East India Company. Uncle James reported to the Collector, Charles Hillersdon, which meant that he was one of the officials who travelled around the vast district collecting taxes. Apart from these journeys around the countryside, on which he often took Hari, it was not an exacting job and Uncle James had not kept himself in good condition. He was a large man to begin with, but the extra fat he carried made him look like a huge, slow-moving bear. His face was permanently red and sported a sprawling mustache and wide, mutton chop side whiskers. He seemed continually out of breath and always dressed in a formal suit to "maintain appearances." The main consequence was that Jack had never seen his uncle not bathed in sweat. It stood out now on his fleshy face and ran in tiny rivers down his cheeks and neck to disappear beneath the stiff collar of his shirt.

"Got to break the cartridge paper to load. Otherwise the damned gunpowder won't light," he explained. "Biting the top off's the fastest way, always has been. Problem is, these new Enfield muskets have grooves down the inside of the barrels. Apparently, it makes 'em more accurate—greater range and so forth—but it makes the cartridge a tight fit. Got to grease the cartridge to get it down the barrel."

"But why won't they bite them?" Jack continued.

"Some silliness about the grease being cow fat or pig fat or some such. They refuse to bite the cartridges because it will defile them."

"But it will," Jack exclaimed, remembering his conversations with Hari. "Cows are sacred to Hindus and pigs are unclean to Muslims."

"Which only goes to show the primitive nature of the religions these fellows hold to. The *sepoys* are soldiers and must do as they are ordered. Otherwise the army'll fall apart. If they're ordered to bite the cartridges then bite them they must, cow fat or no."

"But—"

Uncle James held up a hand to prevent Jack's interruption. "Besides, they have been assured that the grease is from sheep. Some regiments have even been allowed to tear off the top of the cartridge rather than bite it. But still the nonsense goes on. Look what happened at Barrackpore in March."

"What?"

"Oh, some chap, Pande his name was, attacked his officers. Been smoking too much opium, if you ask me."

"But what did that have to do with the cartridges?" Jack encouraged his uncle.

"Well, this Pande claimed to have been incited to revolt by others who were afraid of losing their caste through biting the greased cartridges. Nothing was ever proved, but it's odd, not one of the regiment went to their European officer's aid, at least until they were threatened with being shot themselves. Disgraceful."

"What happened to Pande?"

"He was hanged of course, and his entire regiment disbanded. Far too lenient, if you ask me. There has been trouble in other places, too, over the last few months—strange affairs. Needs a firm hand. A few *sepoys* blown from the mouths of the regimental cannons will stop all this nonsense."

"That's barbaric," Jack said, shocked.

"Barbaric? We're not the barbarians here, Jack, and discipline must be maintained. It's the only thing these fellows understand. Let one away with something and they all want to try. They're like a lot of children."

"But you wouldn't blow a naughty child from the mouth of a cannon!"

"It's not the same." An angry tone entered Uncle James's voice. "You are new here. You don't understand how things are done. When you've been here as long as I have, you will see things the way I do."

"I doubt I will ever think it is right to blow men from cannons just because they feel their religion is threatened."

"This conversation is at an end." Uncle James pushed his chair back and rose. The servant who had stood behind him throughout the meal jumped back to avoid being hit.

"Katherine, see what you can do with this boy. I was perfectly prepared to take him in after your brother died, even if he is a half-caste, but I will not have him tell me I am wrong at my own dinner table. I am going to lie down."

As Uncle James moved his large, sweaty bulk out of the room, he drew with him a flurry of scuttling servants.

"Don't worry about him," Aunt Katherine advised Jack. "The heat always bothers him. But he does have a point. A year is not a long time to get used to this country. You still have a lot to learn about how things are done. All that separates us from the savages is continuing to do things in the proper way. We must maintain appearances. You will see that eventually."

Jack doubted he would but he didn't want to argue with his aunt as well. "I think I'll go and find Hari and practise my Hindi."

A worried look crossed his aunt's face. "Don't spend too much time with that boy."

"Why not? He's teaching me things."

"Yes, and learning is good, but he is an Indian and you are not. It will be difficult enough for you to fit in here with your colour of skin. If you spend too much time with the likes of the stable boy, word will spread that you have gone native and that lets everyone down."

Jack frowned. Suddenly, he felt the urge to explain that he didn't *want* to fit in with Aunt Katherine's world. It was Hari's world—with its exotic customs and traditions—that interested him. He opened his mouth to speak, but changed his mind. He was too hot and, in any case, it would do no good. Aunt Katherine was as set in her ways as Uncle James.

"I'll be careful," was all he said as he stood and retreated outside onto the verandah.

The heat hit Jack like a physical presence. It sucked the air from his lungs and the moisture from his skin, yet somehow it was less stifling than the cooler dining room he had shared with his aunt and uncle. Gasping, Jack moved round to the back of the house where Hari sat waiting for him.

"*Namaste*, Hari." Jack placed his palms together and greeted his friend.

"Good afternoon, Jack Sahib," Hari replied, nodding his head. "How was your morning ride?"

"Very good, thank you, Hari. I met someone."

Hari inclined his head enquiringly.

Jack hesitated. He desperately wanted to talk about the strange girl he had met and how he felt about her, but was Hari the right person to confide in? He was a friend, but he was also a servant. Was it appropriate to talk about personal things with a servant? Clearly, Aunt Katherine and Uncle James didn't think so. For the moment, Jack gave up trying to sort things out. He simply said, "She told me the story of the Bibighar."

"Indeed, that is a most sad tale, sahib. Now, what is it you wish us to be learning today?"

"I wish you would learn to stop calling me sahib." Jack sat down on the wooden floor. "I'm Jack, not Jack Sahib."

"But it is a term of politeness and of respect."

"Then I should call you Hari Sahib."

Hari looked shocked. "No, Jack Sahib. I am but a lowly stable boy."

"And I am just a half-caste orphan from Canada West."

"But you are of the Raj. You are a ruler and deserving of respect."

34

Jack gave up. Some things about this country couldn't be changed.

"I remember some Hindi my mother taught me—
Humpty Dumpty bita me chat
Humpty Dumpty girgea fat
Rajah kigora
Ranee kinora
Humpty Dumpty cabinae jora."

Hari looked puzzled. "It makes little sense, Jack Sahib."

Jack laughed. "I know. It's not supposed to. It's about an egg that fell off a wall."

"Why would a Rajah wish to mend a broken egg?"

"Actually, it wasn't originally about an egg at all. Humpty Dumpty was a battering ram in a war in England many years ago. It was built to break down a city's walls but it got stuck in a river and broke. Hundreds of soldiers died."

"Why would your mother sing songs to a child about soldiers dying?"

"It's not about soldiers dying. It's a nursery rhyme."

"The English are very strange. I do not think I shall ever be understanding them."

"Sometimes I don't understand them either," Jack said with a smile. "But there is something I don't understand here. Do you know about the new greased cartridges?"

Hari's face went serious. "I do, Jack Sahib. It is not good."

"You are always telling me things are not good, but I want to know more. Why are the *sepoys* refusing to bite the cartridges if they are not cow fat?"

"They are not trusting officers."

"But why not? Many of the officers I have met are devoted to their men. They wouldn't lie to them."

"What you are saying is true. I knew one such in Lucknow before I came here one year ago—a Captain Moore. He was a most goodly man. From his own pocket, he was paying for me to go to school and learn the English. But many *badmashes*—undesirable persons of low character—from the bazaar have been spreading stories."

"What kind of stories?"

"They say the big war in the Crimea killed all the British soldiers in England. There are none left but the few that are here and they could easily be killed."

"That's nonsense. There are thousands of soldiers still in England."

Hari nodded his head enigmatically. "They are also saying that, because there are no soldiers left in England, the Little Queen will be sending all the young women to India to marry Brahmin men, rob them of their caste and turn them into Christians."

"But that's crazy!"

"These are most difficult times. There is much craziness. Yesterday there was a holy man in the bazaar—a *fakir*—who talked most loudly of swords draped in gore and rooms full of blood. He was saying the *feringhees* would all soon be dead and India would be free once more. Many listened."

"*Feringhees*?"

"You, sahib. All foreigners."

Jack could picture the *fakir*; they were a common sight. Often they were naked and filthy, covered in white river clay and ashes. Their hair was long and matted with dirt and, Jack imagined, almost alive with all kinds of bugs. But the *fakirs* were revered. They had renounced all worldly things and devoted their lives to spiritual enlightenment. It was unusual for them to talk, let alone preach to a crowd.

"Why do they want us to leave? Aren't we helping India become civilized?"

Hari shrugged. "The Vedas say that India was civilized while the *feringhees* still lived in caves."

"Vedas?"

"The ancient books, sahib. They are so old no one knows who wrote them."

"Do you want us to leave, Hari?"

"It is good to control one's destiny."

"But if the British had not come here, you would not have gone to school."

"That is most true, but it was the kindness of one man, Captain Moore, that enabled my education, and there are good men among all peoples."

"So you want us gone."

"One day in peace. Not now in war. The British are not the worst of masters. I am not thinking that Nana Sahib is someone to be wished for."

Jack was fascinated. This was as close as he had come to finding out how Hari felt about something and it might be a chance to express his own mixed feelings about the country. Despite the strangeness of the land, Jack was finding it more and more difficult to think of himself as a foreigner. He opened his mouth to continue the discussion, but Hari stood up.

"I must be attending to the horses. Thank you for this talk, Jack Sahib, it was a most interesting conversation."

Jack shook his head as he watched Hari retreat across the garden. Despite all the time he spent in Hari's company, India was still a mystery. Jack couldn't help but feel that the land Hari described to him was nothing but a surface veneer that covered a wild and turbulent history stretching back into an unimaginably distant past.

Tuesday, May 12—Evening

The vultures sat in the regimented rows of trees beside the road like black-shawled prophets of doom. From their hunched shoulders, obscenely bald heads stretched forward on stringy necks and hungry eyes watched Jack as he rode past in the dusty evening light.

There was so much death in this land, Jack reflected, that the animals that lived off it—vultures and jackals on the land and crocodiles in the river—thrived. The first two didn't bother him much, although their activities sometimes disgusted him. It was the crocodiles he feared. Everyone seemed to delight in telling him stories of people standing in waist-deep water suddenly screaming and disappearing beneath the surface. He had even heard of buffalo being dragged in while they were drinking. The thought of such a horrible fate coming at him unseen from beneath the brown water of the Ganges sent shivers down his spine. He much preferred the vultures along the road.

The Grand Trunk Road was quiet at this time of day. Gone was the bustle and noise of traders' bullock carts, the clank and rattle of military columns, and the otherworldly shuffle of the skinny *fakirs*. Farmers made their way across the landscape toward mud-brick villages where thin columns of smoke already rose from cooking fires. The hubbub of India was quieting for a few hours.

Jack thought back over the day: the chapattis; the mysterious, beautiful girl at the Bibighar; the greased cartridges; Hari's story of the unrest in the bazaar. There was no pattern to it, yet Jack felt a curious unease, as if something unpleasant were about to happen. He had heard stories of the village dogs acting oddly hours before an earthquake struck, as if they somehow sensed that the solid earth beneath them was about to act in a strange and dangerous way. Perhaps Jack was sensing some horrible wrench in the fabric of the ordered life of British India.

Nonsense. Jack shook his head to dispel his wild imaginings. It was just another evening, and a lovely one at that. Evening was Jack's favourite time, but it was too short. In front of him, at the end of the tunnel of trees, the sun—blood red and huge—sat on the flat horizon, preparing to plunge the world into darkness.

Jack didn't think he would ever get used to the speed with which the Indian day turned into night. One minute the sun was beating down with malevolent fury and he had to squint against its harsh glare. Then it was gone. There was a brief softening of the light, a short period of semi-dark and suddenly the stars leapt out of the blackness. It was all so different from the long gentle twilights he was used to in Canada West where the day seemed to pass regretfully into night.

Thoughts of cool evening rides through the Canadian woods with a brace of grouse or a small deer thrown over the saddle in front of him tugged at Jack's emotions. Not a day went past when he didn't achingly miss that earlier life—the quiet woods and empty spaces that were the opposite of this strident, teeming land. He felt sharp tears sting the corners of his eyes. It wasn't fair! Why did his parents have to die? Why did he have to be sent off to this alien place where vultures were as common as crows?

Jack had always been a loner. There hadn't been much choice in sparsely populated Canada West, but here he felt alone in the middle of thousands of people. He had so little in common with any of them. Sometimes he enjoyed that, taking pride in being different, but deep down he knew the real reason for his lonely existence was the colour of his skin.

Most European women and children in India kept out of the sun and treasured an alabaster complexion. Jack's skin marked him as Eurasian—a half-caste, destined never to completely fit in with either society. But then so was the girl he had met this morning. Perhaps the two of them—

"'Ey, Jackie boy! 'Old up." A strong cockney accent of London's east end broke into Jack's dreams, making him rein in. Coming up the road was a soldier. He wore the red uniform of a subaltern in the 53rd Native Infantry Regiment and he was mounted on a cavalry horse, much larger than Australian.

"Hello, Tommy," Jack said with a smile as the man drew level.

Tommy Davies was seven years older than Jack but he looked more. Almost ten years of army life in the uncompromising climates of India and the Crimea had weathered his skin to the texture of old leather. Only his pale blue eyes, sparkling beneath dark brows, still appeared young.

Tommy was one of the few Europeans in Cawnpore with whom Jack felt a kinship. Like Jack, he didn't fit in. His father owned a fishmonger's shop in London and Tommy himself had a strong accent. This made him "common" and unlike most of the upper-class officers in the Indian Army. Despite the odds, Tommy had done well. As a boy in his father's shop, gutting and cleaning fish at a cold marble slab, Tommy had dreamed of adventure. In 1844, when he was only ten, he ran away from home to join the navy and become a cabin boy on Sir John Franklin's great Arctic adventure. His father caught him before he could sign his life away and Tommy was eternally grateful that he had: not a single member of Franklin's expedition survived to return home from the icy north.

Luckily, Tommy's father recognized that he could not force his son to do what he did not want, so he worked with him—saving every penny and begging favours from his upper-class customers—to get a cadet scholarship to Addiscombe Military College. In the proudest moment of his life so far, Tommy graduated as a subaltern in the summer of 1848, just in time to be shipped to India and contribute to the victory against the Sikhs at the Battle of Chillianwalla the following year. Then there were wars in Burma and the Crimea. Tommy had done a lot of soldiering in a short time.

"Gawd, look at them letters!" Tommy said.

"Look at what?"

"Letters. Letters and words—birds. You don't know

nuffink." Most of the time, Tommy tried hard to hide his accent, but he had particular trouble stopping himself from replacing "th" in the middle of a word with "ff" or dropping the "h" at the beginning of a word. On top of that, he often exaggerated his accent when he was with Jack. He took particular pride in torturing his friend with the impossible to follow rhyming slang that he had grown up with.

"Sometimes," Jack said, shaking his head, "it seems as if you're using a different language. Hindi is easier than that mess you speak."

"I say, old chap," Tommy said, affecting a cultured voice that sounded as if he had a mouthful of plums. "That's a bit thick, what!"

The pair laughed as they set off along the road.

"But seriously," Tommy said, "Those birds give me the creeps. They look as if they know someffing we don't."

"What bothers me," Jack replied, "is that they are so plump. There must be a lot of dead things around to keep this many vultures well fed."

"It's them Hindus, burning bodies down by the river. The poor folk can't afford enough wood to do the job proper, so they just turf what's left into the water. Not often vultures and crocodiles get a cooked meal, eh?"

"That's disgusting!"

"But true. I took a boat down and had a butcher's last week." Tommy smiled at Jack's puzzled frown. "Butcher's hook—look."

"You're not supposed to."

"I know, but everyone does. We got in so close to the pyre that the mourners were starting to wave us away.

Strangest thing—the body in the middle of the blaze sat up."

"What?"

"Sat bolt upright as if it was about to ask for a nice cool drink of water."

"That's not possible," Jack said incredulously.

Tommy laughed. "Captain Moore says it 'appens all the time. Someffing to do with the heat making the tendons contract—jerks the body right up. I tell you, we didn't need any encouragement to scarper after that."

The pair rode in silence for a while as they thought about Tommy's story. Eventually, they turned off onto a dirt track that led past the European barracks to the Sati Chowra Ghat and the Europeans' bungalows.

"Do you like it here?" Jack asked.

"Oh, it ain't the South Downs nor Hyde Park, that's for sure, and it's either dreadfully hot or pouring rain, but there's worse places. Take the Crimea for instance—disease, muddle and nonsense everywhere. If it 'adn't been for the bravery of the common soldier, we'd never 'ave won that war. But at least there was some excitement there, not like 'ere where we sit around in the 'eat and dust sweating our lives away."

"There might be some excitement here yet. There's some strange things happening."

"That's true enough," Tommy responded. "The natives are restless over these new greased cartridges. But, if you ask me, there's always someffing strange in this land. No need to worry, though. The army 'as everyffing under control. 'Sides, General Wheeler says the native regiments are staunch."

"Staunch? Where are you picking up the fancy language? And since when has General Wheeler confided in a fishmonger's son?"

Tommy coloured at the reference to his background. "That's rich coming from an 'alf-caste. I'll 'ave you know that my dad is the best fishmonger in Whitechapel. He supplies fresh fish to the Earl of Sutton Regis."

"All right," Jack said hurriedly, ignoring the dig at his mixed heritage. "Don't get upset. I'm not one of those snobs who's impressed by the Earl of this or that. But you must admit, General Wheeler isn't in the habit of inviting lowly subalterns to tiffin."

Tommy relaxed with a laugh. "True enough, but I didn't 'ear it from 'im. I 'eard it from Captain Moore."

"Who is this Captain Moore everyone seems to be talking about?"

"'E came in with the squad of regulars from Lucknow at the beginning of the month. You must 'ave seen him about—that tall, fair-haired Irishman. Anyway, 'e is the opposite of ol' Wheeler. The ol' general has got cautious in his dotage. Moore is a right firebrand, 'e is. Says we should disarm the *sepoy* regiments before there's any trouble."

"Is there going to be trouble?"

"Naw. It's all just fuss and bother. It'll blow over. But it wouldn't hurt to take precautions."

"Such as?"

"Disarming the regiments, for one. Maybe preparing the magazine on the edge of town for defence. That place is a fortress. With enough food we could hold out there for months."

"Hold out? What are you talking about?"

"Nuffing. Just soldier's talk. We're always preparing for the next battle. Usually never comes. Still an' all, can't hurt to be prepared."

"I'm sure General Wheeler has everything under control."

"I'm sure he 'as," Tommy replied. The two lapsed back into silence.

General Sir Hugh Massey Wheeler was one of the most senior officers in India. In fifty years of service, he had fought against Sikhs and Afghans, and earned the nickname "Attack" for the wild charges he had led in his youth. But he had never been given the high honours and position he warranted in his old age. In the eyes of the fussy establishment, General Wheeler was tainted in much the same way as Jack. The general's wife, Frances, was Eurasian; her father had been white and her mother Indian.

"I met a girl this morning," Jack said.

"Well done, me lad. About time you discovered some delicate flower of the cantonment and settled down. What's 'er name?"

"I don't know. I was riding past the Bibighar and she was sitting on the wall. She told me a story."

"That's very nice," Tommy said. "But 'er name would 'elp."

"She was beautiful."

"Well, that's all right, then. Just put a notice in the *India Gazette*: wanted, beautiful girl to tell stories—piece o' cake."

"You don't take anything seriously, do you?"

"Only proper things to worry about in the army are keeping your powder dry and your boots clean."

Jack burst out laughing.

"What's so funny?"

"Proper was what the story was about," Jack said getting himself under control. "That's Aunt Katherine's favourite word. Meals must be eaten at the proper time, servants must be treated in a proper way and proper clothes must be worn for every occasion." Jack pulled his shoulders back and perfectly mimicked his aunt's high-pitched voice, "Doing the proper thing is what distinguishes us from the savages. Sometimes I despair of ever making anything worthwhile of you, Jack O'Hara. I don't know what my brother, God rest his soul, was thinking. First, he up and marries a *bibi*, and then, as soon as you are born, he takes off to the wilds of the North American colonies. I fear it has ruined you for ever becoming a gentleman. There is too much of the savage in you."

"I've often thought that meself," Tommy said with a smile. "I may be a fishmonger's son, but you are a savage."

"I'm not alone." Jack laughed. "To Aunt Katherine, savages include anyone not brought up in England. I fear I lie too far on the wrong side of the proper-savage line to ever be redeemed."

Tommy pulled out his watch from the fob pocket in his uniform jacket, flipped open the cover and carefully looked at the time. Jack smiled. The sun was setting at the same time as it had last night but Tommy loved his watch and examined it at every opportunity. It had been a gift from his father on his last leave, just before he boarded the boat for India back in January. The outer case was engraved with a hunting scene of hounds bringing down a stag, and Tommy's name and the date of his departure were engraved inside the case. Jack knew how long and hard a fishmonger would have to work to afford a watch like that.

"Do you sleep with that under your pillow?" Jack asked.

"What, me kettle?"

"I know that one," Jack said. "Kettle and hob—fob—watch."

"We'll make a cockney of you yet, me ol' china plate. You see if we don't."

"China plate's mate?" Jack asked, but Tommy was distracted, looking over at a squad of *sepoys* in their red coats and black trousers, lounging beside the track. They saluted Tommy as he rode past.

"They looked staunch," Jack commented with a laugh when they were out of earshot.

"They did," Tommy replied, seriously. "But did you notice? Some of them saluted with their left 'ands. That's a sign of disrespect. I shall 'ave to report them when I return."

"What's all the fuss about these new greased cartridges?" Jack asked. "I've heard the Hindus say the grease is cow fat and will defile them and the Muslims say it is pork grease and against their religion. Are they right?"

"I don't know. The official story is that it's sheep fat, but I don't think it makes any difference. The general's told them they don't have to bite the end off the cartridge to load their muskets, tearing the end off will work just as well. So, nuffing's going to happen. It will all blow over and the dull life of this place will go on forever."

"And you will marry the general's daughter and become just as fossilized as all the rest. Why, you'll even become a mighty general yourself."

"That's my dream—why I joined the army: to become a mighty general like the Duke of Wellington or even ol' Wheeler."

"I don't think a fishmonger's son has ever made general."

"Then I'll be the first. No fishmonger's son ever came first in his class at Addiscombe either—until me. The army's me life. I work 'ard at it. I've read Caesar's *Conquest of Gaul* and von Clausewitz's *On War*. Then, after a long life winning dramatic battles against savage hordes, I will 'ave a Viking funeral."

"Pushed out to sea in a long boat in flames?"

"Yes."

Jack laughed. "You'd spoil it by sitting up and falling off the boat."

Tommy joined in the laughter. "I suppose I would. What's your dream?"

"To discover a lost city like Pompeii," Jack said without hesitation. "I love the idea that there are the remains of ancient civilizations under the ground. There weren't in the Canadas—although I used to collect arrowheads—but my dad gave me a book, Seely's *The Wonders of Elora*. I read it over and over again. It's about discovering the rock-hewn temples outside Bombay. I used to stare at the pictures and imagine myself hacking my way through the jungle and coming upon an overgrown city. It was the one thing

I liked about being sent here; there are lost cities waiting to be found."

"And when I am a general, you can take me on a tour."

They were approaching the European barracks and hospital, two long verandahed mud brick buildings sitting in isolation on the dusty plain east of the main city. This was where Tommy was headed.

"Seems to be a lot of activity this evening," Tommy commented as he squinted in the failing light. Jack noticed figures running around the barrack compound, but thought nothing of it. Military matters were a mystery to him.

As the pair approached the buildings, an officer rode toward them. When he was within hailing distance, he yelled at Tommy, "There's a general alert. Get back to your unit."

"What's the trouble?" Tommy asked.

"Word's just come in from Meerut. The *sepoys* mutinied there two nights ago—killed most of the officers and their families, burned the town and marched on Delhi."

"Gawd!" Tommy exclaimed. He spurred his horse forward and yelled back over his shoulder. "Jack, get back to the bungalow until this is all sorted out."

Jack felt a chill run up his spine. His mind raced back to the mysterious chapattis and the story Hari had told him. Was this the beginning?

PART II

The Vultures Wait

Thursday, May 21

The powerful jaws clamped around Jack's body and dragged him below the water. He struggled frantically but his arms and legs were paralyzed. He knew what was going to happen: the crocodile was dragging him under to drown, then it would take him back to its den in the riverbank to eat at leisure. As the beast hauled him into the dark, muddy hole, Jack realized with utter terror that he hadn't drowned. He was going to be eaten alive!

Suddenly wide awake but still sweating with fear, Jack snapped his body into a sitting position. The clammy sheets wrapped around his arms and legs pulled him awkwardly to the side and he tumbled through the mosquito netting onto the hard floor. A startled green lizard scuttled away and up the wall where it hung, watching curiously. For a moment, Jack lay panting, forcing himself back into reality. Gradually, he pushed the confused memory of the nightmare back into the recesses of his mind.

In the days since the news of the mutiny in Meerut had swept through the town, tales of massacres and murder in Delhi and countless other isolated stations along the Ganges had kept everyone on edge. Terrified refugees had begun to pour into town and yesterday the decomposing body of a white woman, partly torn apart by crocodiles—*muggars*—had drifted slowly past, held afloat by the widespread folds of her blue, sequined ball gown. General Wheeler had issued orders to dig trenches and throw up parapets around the European barracks to create a place of refuge if the worst happened.

Slowly, Jack untangled himself from the damp sheets and stood. The morning heat was already a physical presence, pressing down like a weight and sucking away what little energy he had. The waving *punkah* served only to move the uncomfortably heavy air around the sparsely furnished room.

He walked to the sideboard and splashed his face with some of the warm water in the large china bowl. Then he dressed. He didn't hurry even though he knew he was going to be late for breakfast—he was always late for breakfast. He imagined Aunt Katherine sitting at one end of the long, polished dining table, complaining to her husband at the other end, "He doesn't know how to do things properly."

Jack chuckled to himself. "And look at the state of your clothes!" he spoke aloud, mimicking his aunt's voice as he stood looking at his reflection in the mirror fixed to the back of the door. Jack was a talented mimic and enjoyed using his talent. Of course, it was not something Aunt Katherine approved of. "You look like a native beggar," he continued. "How are we supposed to show that we are superior to the natives if we do not act properly? You are letting the side down, Jack."

"Don't worry, Aunt Katherine," Jack went on in his normal voice, "I'll put on a *dhoti* and go and play with the bazaar children." He burst out laughing as he imagined his aunt's horrified reaction.

Still smiling, Jack turned and caught a glimpse of Hari peering in at the window. He gave a slight nod and broke into a half-apologetic smile before disappearing from sight. Jack shook his head. He would never get used to the almost ghostly presence of the servants—always there, yet invisible when they wanted to be. Jack had tried several times over the past few days to find Hari and talk to him about the mutinies, but his friend was never to be found. Either he was too busy or he was away from the house on some errand. Today, Jack would make a determined effort to find him.

Jack fastened the last button on his already sweat-stained shirt and went through to the dining room where the familiar smell of fried bacon and sausages mingled with the exotic odour of curry and the fresh scent of guavas and papayas. He stopped in the doorway. Everything looked as it should—the table was set with shining silver and crystal, dishes of food were set out in regimented rows on the sideboard, immaculately dressed servants stood to attention along the walls, ready to attend to the diner's slightest need—but there were no diners.

Jack glanced at the grandfather clock in the corner. It *was* past breakfast time and Aunt Katherine was a stickler for punctuality. She would never allow this level of tardiness in her husband or herself. Puzzled, Jack was about to ask one of the servants if the memsahib was ill when his aunt bustled through the wide double doors that led out onto the verandah. Jack had the impression of a storm of lace and crinoline blowing in from the garden. Her green skirts and rustling layers of petticoats billowed out from her waist, above which her thin, corseted body perched.

"There you are," she said as she swept past without even a glance at the waiting food. "It's all such a nuisance. Hurry along and pack now."

"Pack?"

"Yes, pack." Jack's aunt stopped and turned to stare at her nephew. She was shorter than him, but she looked up with a pair of sharp, dark eyes set beneath precise eyebrows. Her nose was hooked, giving her whole face a bird-like appearance, and her skin was as white as snow in a Canadian winter. A vague scent of lavender wafted around Jack.

"Haven't you heard? There was some silly disturbance among the native troops last night. Several houses were set on fire. It's nothing—these natives are always squabbling among themselves—but James feels that it is time for us all to move into the military barracks. I think it's a mistake. We must not show weakness at a time like this, it will merely encourage the bad elements—appearance is everything. Still, we have been told to move and we must stick together. Now, James will be round with the carriage in half an hour. You are to pack one bag of clothes—I have told the stable boy to help you. Now move along."

In a whisper of petticoats, Aunt Katherine swept out of the dining room, leaving Jack feeling stunned. Was mutiny about to break out here despite all General Wheeler's confidence? Jack grabbed a couple of sausages and some rashers of bacon before heading out of the dining room. "Thank you," he said to the nearest impassive servant.

Jack was surprised to find Hari already in his room. He was busy folding Jack's clothes and packing them into a large canvas roll that doubled as bedding for travelling.

"It's all right, Hari. I'll pack," Jack said in Hindi.

Hari's head bobbed an enigmatic reply. "Memsahib say pack," he said in English.

"I know, Hari, but I would rather pack myself."

Again the nod of the head. Hari retreated toward the door.

"Hari, wait. Do you know anything about the fires last night?" Jack reverted to English.

Hari turned and looked at Jack. For a moment, their eyes met and Jack suddenly thought how rare it was for an Indian to meet his gaze. "*Badmashes*," Hari said.

"The troublemakers from the bazaar?"

"Yes. Yes. Troublemakers."

"So, it wasn't the *sepoys* who set the fires?"

For a moment Hari hesitated, giving Jack the fleeting sense that he was deciding what pieces of information to give out. Perhaps it was just his command of English, Jack thought, searching for a simpler explanation, but thanks to the mysterious Captain Moore, Hari had received an excellent education. He rarely stumbled over his English—and why had Moore paid for Hari's education anyway? More questions and no real answers. Jack opened his mouth to ask about the captain, but Hari spoke first, bringing Jack's mind back to more immediate concerns.

"The memsahib is most correct. You must be going with all speed to the entrenchment. *Badmashes* very much say *feringhees,* time over. Much trouble." Hari's eyes took on a pleading expression.

"I'll go," Jack agreed. Instantly, Hari looked relieved. "But not in the carriage with the sahib and memsahib. Could you saddle Australian and bring him round to the front? I will ride to the barracks. Please let the memsahib know."

Hari nodded and left.

One advantage to having servants, Jack reflected, was that you didn't have to run around telling people what you were doing. You could always ask a servant to relay the news, which was a significant benefit if you wanted to do something that they wouldn't approve of.

Jack finished gathering his clothes and dragged his roll out onto the front verandah. Noises of packing were coming from throughout the house and several servants hurried past, but Jack was relieved to see no sign of Aunt Katherine. Sweating in the heat, he carried his bedroll to the roadside.

The main street through the cantonment was busier than Jack had ever seen. The air was filled with the rattle and clank of harnesses and bits and the thump of hooves as bored horses stamped impatiently while harried servants loaded belongings onto carts. Some carriages were already full and rumbled past in clouds of dust, precious belongings swaying precariously on top. Jack had glimpses of pale, frightened faces peering out from behind curtained windows.

All at once, the enormity what was happening struck

him with the force of a cannonball. Aunt Katherine's matter-of-fact manner had given the impression of going on a picnic—but this was a full-scale flight. Everyone was running away, abandoning their houses, furniture and most of their possessions to an uncertain future. As soon as the cantonment was deserted, it would be only a matter of hours before the looters moved in. This was much more serious than Jack had realized.

As if to underline the point, a large carriage rushed past, dangerously close to where Jack stood. The blond heads of two small boys—twins, Jack wondered?—were framed in one of the windows and, from inside, he could hear the wailing of an infant. One of the boys stuck his tongue out at Jack.

Jack was on the point of returning to the bungalow to go to the barracks with his aunt and uncle when Hari appeared leading Australian. Now, suddenly, it was difficult to change his mind without looking silly.

"Thank you," he said, taking the bridle from Hari and mounting. Almost at once he felt stronger and more confident. Australian was comfortingly steady beneath him and his lofty perch gave the feeling of being above the panic. He looked down at Hari. "Will you come to the barracks?"

"I think, no. I will be of greater use outside."

"What do you mean, 'greater use outside'?"

Hari looked startled. "The memsahib," he said abruptly, "most clearly wishes that I stay and guard the bungalow from *badmashes*. That is all I was meaning."

There it was again, the feeling that there was something more beneath the surface Hari presented to the world. Jack wanted to ask him more—to get at what Hari was really thinking—but he didn't know how to begin. "Be careful."

Hari nodded. "And you take much care also."

Then Hari was gone. Pondering the odd encounter, Jack gently prodded Australian into motion and set off down the road at a trot.

The most direct route to the military barracks lay close to the native city and bazaar, and several hundred people had come out to watch the ramshackle column of refugees pass. Jack rode on, travelling through a sea of dark, skinny, upturned faces. Some thin lips were pulled back over surprisingly large white teeth as the mouths screamed insults. Other faces were passive with brown eyes watching almost regretfully.

Sweetmeat sellers—*halwis*—shuffled through the crowd, offering their wares, their monotonous cries competing with the high-pitched, pleading whines of the beggars demanding alms or rice. The background hum of hundreds of voices almost drowned out the creaking of the wooden carts and the rattle of their iron-rimmed wheels on the stony road. The exotic smells of spices mixed with the cloying odour of open toilets and the harsh dust thrown up by the procession. Behind the crowd, carpets of fiery red chillies lay in the sun to dry and tubs of brightly coloured dyes almost gave the occasion a festive air.

Squads of red-clad soldiers, their long bayonets glinting in the sun, provided some security, but Jack couldn't get over a feeling of smallness. India was so vast and her people so numerous that it was impossible to believe that a few thousand British could rule without her consent. If India ever organized and became united, she could sweep the *feringhees* into the ocean as easily as Jack could sweep a handful of ants off a tabletop.

It was a disturbing thought; one Jack had not had before. Despite his Eurasian heritage and his thoughts of rebellion against the thoughtless superiority of his aunt and uncle, he was a part of the ruling class—the fabled British Raj that lorded over India and her multitudes as securely as the Mughal Emperors had in the past. The argument was always that Britain was "civilizing the nation" and bringing it all the benefits of modern technology, but what if that were not true? What if the East India Company merely ruled the subcontinent for profit and didn't care what happened to the people? What if 170 million Indians had finally realized this and decided to do something about it?

Jack remembered being told stories about the MacKenzie and Papineau revolts in Upper and Lower Canada in 1837. Although the revolts had failed, they had happened because many people felt that the powerful men who controlled the country did not listen to them. What if it was the same in India, but on a much larger scale?

A carriage pulled up alongside Jack, interrupting his thoughts. It was a large four-wheeler, surrounded by immaculately turned out cavalrymen and drawn by a matching pair of horses that dwarfed Australian. As Jack glanced at it, the curtain parted and a pair of dark, almond eyes looked out at the chaotic world around with interest and no fear. With a gasp, Jack recognized the beautiful girl from the Bibighar.

The girl looked directly at Jack and smiled, giving him a glimpse of small, delicate teeth between full lips. Then an arm appeared from the dark interior and closed the curtain, and the carriage left Jack behind.

Obviously, the girl came from a very well-off family. Suddenly Jack felt thrilled at the thought of everyone fleeing to the entrenchment. Soon, he would be cooped up in a confined space with the girl from the Bibighar! It would be easy to find out who she was and, perhaps, engineer another meeting. Maybe this crisis wasn't so bad after all.

Jack arrived at the entrenchment around the barracks exhausted and sweat covered, but relieved to be somewhere secure. His joy at seeing the girl again had faded fast. The hatred in the screaming faces around the straggling refugees had shocked him. All it would take would be a single excuse, one nervous soldier firing wildly into the crowd, and the mob would surge forward and everyone would be overwhelmed in a mass of swinging fists and clubs. But Jack's relief soon turned to dismay. Even to his unpractised eye, the entrenchment looked woefully weak.

A three-foot-high mud wall formed an irregular rectangle eight hundred feet long by four hundred feet wide. It looked to Jack as if it had been laid out by a drunk, bulging out in places to include small buildings and receding back to provide clear fields of fire over the surrounding open plain. Even with the small trench behind it, it looked frighteningly frail.

At least the two barrack buildings enclosed by the mud wall looked sturdy. Both had walls almost two feet thick and ran parallel to the long axis of the entrenchment. The larger, the hospital, was three hundred and fifty feet long by sixty wide and had a thatched roof that looked like a fire hazard to Jack. The other was roofed with tiles, but measured only one hundred and ninety feet long by fifty wide. Both consisted of several rooms arranged along the long axis and flanked by a double verandah designed to keep the interior cool. They seemed deplorably inadequate wartime accommodation for the thousand soldiers, civil employees, women and children who were flocking to them.

"Welcome to General Wheeler's entrenchment."

Jack looked down to see Tommy standing nearby. He dismounted and approached his friend. "Will this place stand up to an attack?"

"Well, it ain't the Tower of London, that's for sure, but we'll manage. The *sepoys* 'aven't mutinied yet. All that fuss is just the bad elements in the bazaar looking for some plunder. And, only the civilians will be in 'ere for the time being. We brave officers will remain in the native barracks with our men. Mind, I'd prefer that we were in the magazine on the other side of town, that's a good solid brick building, much more like a fort."

"Why aren't we?"

"The general didn't want to provoke trouble by fortifying the place and 'e wants to be on this side of town to meet the reinforcements from Allahabad. Besides, nuffing will 'appen. Nana Sahib has given 'is word."

Jack thought back to his conversation with Hari about the chapattis. Perhaps Nana Sahib was not as harmless as he had assumed. In any case, if he was going to lead a mutiny of the *sepoys*, he would hardly announce it beforehand. Before Jack could say anything else, Tommy continued. "But I can't stop and jaw with you now, there's work to do. If I was you, I would hurry into the tiled barracks and find yourself some floor before it fills up completely."

As Tommy turned back to his duties, Jack tethered Australian and made his way through the throng.

Despite the double verandah, the inside rooms of the barracks were stiflingly hot, and they were filling up fast. Jack managed to stake out a square of floor against one wall and protect it until his aunt arrived. She appeared eventually, dressed in a billowing skirt and leading a train of burdened servants.

"This is a disgrace," she announced as she pushed past already settled families toward her nephew. "Is this the best you could do? We'll never fit our possessions in that small area, and I brought only the essentials."

As the servant behind Aunt Katherine staggered under the weight of a huge box of dishes and cutlery, Jack wondered how his aunt defined essential. But he confined himself to pointing out that, in the circumstances, they were lucky to have space in an inside room. Already the outer verandahs were filling up and they would be horribly uncomfortable, exposed as they were to the dust-laden winds of the hot season.

"Well, I think it's all ridiculous anyway," Aunt Katherine went on without a pause or a thank you. "Here we are, running away like a flock of frightened sheep as soon as the rabble burns a few huts. I don't know what this country is coming to."

As his aunt blethered on with her litany of complaints, Jack spread out his bedroll and slipped away to explore the entrenchment. The first thing he noticed was that, even in the near panic of the flight, the social order was being maintained. Officer's families and important civilians occupied the centre rooms. Merchants filled the inner verandah and the outer was overflowing with the Eurasian community. I should be here, Jack thought, but he wasn't about to volunteer to change places with anyone.

Jack strolled past the solitary well to the thatched barracks. Here, the outside verandahs were equally crowded, but the inside rooms were being kept as a hospital and the floor was busy with feverish soldiers on straw bales, the inevitable consequence of life in this unhealthy climate. Even though it wasn't overcrowded, the smell of sickness and the groans and shouts of the delirious men encouraged Jack to retreat rapidly.

Outside the buildings, the compound was filled with stamping horses and untidy piles of discarded possessions. Jack was amazed at what some people had attempted to bring in with them: boxes of books, writing desks, crockery, chairs, even a bed. If these people needed all this, they wouldn't last five minutes where Jack grew up, let alone this pitiful fort if it were ever attacked.

Jack raised his head and looked around. He could easily see over the mud wall in any direction. Dry, brown earth spread out. Looking back the way he had come, Jack could see the bulk of St. John's Church and a few scattered bungalows. Turning slowly, he spotted the riding school, the partially built new barracks and the thatched houses of the native infantry lines. Then a frightening thought struck him—if he could see all these buildings, then someone in them could see him just as easily. If it came to a siege, every square inch of open ground in the entrenchment would be visible to countless rebels with muskets or cannons. Hoping fervently that it wouldn't come to that, Jack returned to see if Aunt Katherine had organized their spot to her satisfaction.

Friday, June 5

D o you think they will attack?" Jack stood beside Tommy in the shallow trench, peering over the low parapet toward the European cantonment where fire crackled hungrily through the thatch of a dozen bungalows. The air was filled with the acrid smell of smoke, and the sound of hoarse yells and musket shots echoed across the plain. Wild dancing shapes were silhouetted against the flames.

After two weeks of uncomfortable inactivity in the dry heat of the overcrowded entrenchment, the excitement was almost a relief. Uncertainty had sapped everyone's strength. Some days the mood in the entrenchment had been buoyant—people discussed how many days until the relief column arrived, chided each other for fleeing so readily at the first sign of trouble and made plans to move back to their bungalows and chastise their servants if the places had not been suitably kept up. On other days, usually after news arrived of some new outrage upriver, the mood was more desolate—people worried that the relief column hadn't arrived yet, discussed who among the servants could be trusted and fretted that they hadn't buried the family silver deeply enough in the bungalow garden.

But everything had changed last night. At the sound of the musket shots, the inhabitants had streamed out of the barracks, bleary-eyed from sleep, to see what the commotion was about. Now, in the smoke and flames of their homes, at least some of the uncertainty was gone. No one would be going back to their bungalows for some time. But was this a full-scale mutiny? Certainly, the *sowars* of the 2nd Cavalry had mutinied and run amok, looting and burning through the night. Many *sepoys* of the 56th Native Infantry had joined them, but the 53rd stood in plain view in the dawn light on their parade ground. Perhaps they could be used to get the unruly elements back under control. But what if they couldn't, or wouldn't? What if they too joined the mutiny? Jack's questions lurked at the back of everyone's mind.

"The general is convinced that they will simply loot the town and march off to Delhi to join the mutineers there," Tommy replied.

"I hope he's right, but your general has been wrong before. They," Jack waved his arm toward the figures dancing in the glow of the conflagration, "don't seem too staunch."

Jack felt oddly ambivalent about the men who were, probably at this very minute, ransacking his aunt and uncle's home. On the one hand, he was relieved that something was finally happening; on the other, he felt oddly removed from it all. He had always thought of himself as an outsider in the world of the European cantonment—

now he watched its destruction with detachment. If the rioters finished their work and rode away, Jack's life would go on. This would be little more than another hiccup in an already tragic and tortuous year. But, if the riot developed into a full-scale mutiny and the *sepoys* launched a concerted attack on the entrenchment? That would be different. Then Jack, along with everyone else behind the pitiful mud walls, would be fighting for his very life.

Jack's thoughts were interrupted by a cannon's boom. A round shot tore through a hut to the left of the parading *sepoys* of the 53rd. The lines wavered but stood firm. A second shot soared over their heads to no greater effect, but when a third bounced directly toward them, the *sepoys* broke formation and dispersed in all directions. Jack was about to ask Tommy what was going on when a voice behind him made him turn.

"It's insane."

It was the girl from the Bibighar. Jack had occasionally seen her in the crowd of the entrenchment, but never close at hand and always when she was surrounded by servants or bustling women. But here she was, alone and not four feet from him. The girl was dressed in a practical riding skirt and blouse and wore a wide-brimmed sun hat. She was standing in full view on the dusty ground behind the trench.

"Best take cover, ma'am," Tommy said respectfully.

"Why?" she asked aggressively, looking down at the two friends. "Do you think our cannons will fire on me too?"

"No," Tommy said hesitantly, "but the mutineers—"

"Mutineers that we have just made," she interrupted.

"Beg pardon?" Tommy asked.

"Last night, the only mutineers were the *sowars* of the 2nd Cavalry. They could have easily been driven off if the officers had held the 56th and 53rd firm, but they abandoned them to hide in the entrenchment." The girl glared down at Tommy who blushed furiously and looked hard at his boots.

"Even after that, the 53rd resisted the calls to join the mutiny and formed up, completely leaderless, to await orders. And what do we do? Fire on them. It's insane."

"They were loyal?" Jack blurted out.

"'Were' is the operative word."

"So why did we fire on them?"

"Apparently, it was felt that the gunners in the entrenchment needed to be committed more securely to our cause. They were ordered to fire on the 53rd to prove their loyalty."

"That's insane," Jack said.

The girl smiled. "I believe that is what I said to begin with. And see how effective the policy has been." She pointed to the east where the native artillerymen were streaming over the parapet and running across the open ground. "We're not even firing on them."

Jack was horrified at her suggestion. "You can't shoot unarmed men in the back when they are running away."

"And I suppose you believe that the seven hundred women and children in here are perfectly safe too? After all, it is not the done thing to harm helpless noncombatants."

"I . . . I don't know." Jack was confused. This was not how ladies spoke, even in Canada West.

"You don't know," the girl went on, "because you don't think. That's the trouble with the whole Empire. No one thinks. People just do things because they have always been done that way or because it is the proper way to do them. We are human beings with brains and free will, yet we try our damnedest not to use them."

Jack was struggling to think of an intelligent response. Perhaps in a calm parlour he would be able to come up with something, but here, in the middle of what was rapidly becoming a full-scale mutiny, his mind was a whirling mass of contradictions.

"Someone's coming!" a voice yelled.

Jack looked over the parapet to see a lone figure on horseback urging his mount toward them. He was out in the open, about six hundred yards away, but figures were running between the huts behind him.

"It's Murphy, the railway man," Tommy said.

"Come on," someone encouraged.

A volley of musket fire rang out from the *sepoy* lines. Murphy flew out of his saddle and crashed to the ground. As his riderless horse jumped the mud wall, Murphy's body twitched a couple of times and lay still.

"How could they do that?" the girl asked, her voice heavy with sarcasm. "Shoot an unarmed man in the back." She spun on her heel and stalked back to the tiled barracks. Tommy and Jack stood, mouths gaping, as she pushed her way through the throng of women and children.

Jack's mind was in turmoil, filled with the image of the girl, eyes afire, declaiming about the state of the Empire. She was smart, and so beautiful.

"You know," Tommy mused. "I think I'd feel happier if she was in command rather than the old general."

"But she's a woman!" Jack said, shocked. "It's not a woman's place to command. A woman's place is in the home."

"Maybe," Tommy conceded, "but as my ol' man used to say, 'a fish don't care what colour the skin is of the hand that guts it.' I suspect that girl would recognize guts when she saw them. And the old general's not the same man who led wild cavalry charges in the First Sikh War. Ask yourself: why are we not in the more defensible magazine, why did we not disarm the *sepoys* at the first sign of trouble as Captain Moore suggested and why did we fire on the only loyal native troops for fifty miles? That girl may not 'ave any military training but, still an' all, she 'as more metal in her than 'er father."

"Her father?"

"Don't you know who that was?"

"It was the girl I met at the Bibighar."

Tommy burst out laughing. "That was Alice Wheeler. You, my lad, have fallen in love with the general's daughter."

Jack stared at his friend in shock. It made sense, the expensive carriage, the knowledge of what was going on, the olive-dark skin—Lady Wheeler was Eurasian. Fantasies of their idyllic life together faded abruptly from Jack's mind. She was so far above him socially it was a miracle she had spoken to him at all. She was as unattainable as if she was a Brahmin and he, an untouchable.

"You look like a fish that's been gutted. You mean to say you really 'ad no idea that was Alice Wheeler? Why, every young buck in the officers' mess would give ten years' promotion to pay a call on 'er, but she 'as none of it. Oh, she fills 'er dance card but she makes them keep a good distance. I suspect they run a mile as soon as gives 'em a broadside on the iniquities of the workhouse or the Chartist revolt. My fellow officers are not noted for their intellect nor liberal tendencies."

"There they go!" a voice yelled.

Jack dragged his gaze up to see the 53rd streaming through Cawnpore toward the Delhi road.

"Maybe ol' Wheeler was right after all," Tommy said. "They're legging it off to Delhi. All we have to do now is sit and wait for the relief column. Then we can send the women and children down to Calcutta and get on with teaching these mutineers a lesson they won't soon forget.

"But I must go and see to the arrangements for our defence until then. Don't go wooing any strange women while I am gone."

Jack only grunted in reply as he slumped down against the trench wall. He needed time to think. There had been too many shocks for one morning.

—

By afternoon, an unearthly silence hung like a pall over the city. Several men went to investigate how their bungalows had fared in the riot and returned to report the city quiet with only merchants and servants present, all of them eager to convince anyone who would listen of their continuing loyalty. Murphy's bloodstained body was recovered and hurriedly buried in St. John's churchyard. A squad of soldiers recovered several barrels of rum and beer, and brought them into the entrenchment. Like everyone else, Jack waited. He had almost got used to the idea that the girl was Alice Wheeler and could rationally accept that they were doomed to live in separate worlds, yet tiny fragments of an impossible fantasy life together kept creeping into his mind.

In the late afternoon, Jack met his uncle by the well in the centre of the entrenchment.

"Well," Uncle James wheezed at his nephew, "we have fared better than those poor devils at Meerut and Delhi. In a day or two the relief will be here and we can get on with our lives. Be a good chap and trot over and see how the bungalow is. I spotted some smoke from that direction. I hope it wasn't our place. I left all the paperwork there and its loss would be dreadful."

Jack refrained from pointing out that Murphy's death was dreadful and asking why, if the paperwork was so important, Uncle James had brought his wardrobe trunk and Aunt Katherine's crockery into the entrenchment instead. He merely nodded and went to untether Australian.

Jack was quite happy to perform the task for Uncle James. The entrenchment was crowded and boring. Perhaps, if the bungalow was all right, they could move back tomorrow.

Jack had just trotted past St. John's churchyard where a fresh mound of earth marked Murphy's grave when a low whistle caught his attention. Peering around, he spotted a figure hunched in the shadows of the church wall.

"Hari. Is that you?"

The figure nodded.

Jack dismounted and, tying Australian to the gate post, approached. "What are you doing here?"

"Quick, young sahib, you must be taking message back to General Wheeler Sahib."

"Message?" Jack was thoroughly confused. Why would Aunt Katherine's stable boy want him to take a message to General Wheeler?

"Tell the General Sahib that Nana Sahib has sacked the treasury and he goes, even now, on the Delhi road on his royal elephant to bring his army back to destroy you all."

Jack's mind was reeling. What was Hari talking about?

"What do you mean? I am going back to see how the bungalow is."

"Bungalow gone," Hari hissed urgently. "Go tell."

"How do you know all this?"

"I work for Captain Moore."

Jack's stomach gave a lurch. Suddenly, his world seemed to be spinning out of control. "Captain Moore?"

"Yes, Jack Sahib. Why was it you were thinking he sent me to such a fine English school? Captain Moore is running an establishment of many men and boys such as I. We watch and we listen and we measure and we are telling Captain Moore what is happening so that he can report it all to the Little Queen back in her great palace in England."

"You're a spy?"

Hari's head bobbed enigmatically.

"How? Why?" Jack floundered helplessly.

"There is not being enough time now," Hari said. "You must be taking message to General Sahib."

Then Hari was gone, a hunched figure darting around the building toward the bazaar.

Jack stood immobile. All the things he had struggled to understand since his arrival in India were being undermined. Nothing was as it seemed. The rigid structure of European society had been torn apart in bloody mutiny, the boredom of having to do things in the proper way had been replaced by a violent struggle for survival and Aunt Katherine's stable boy was actually a spy.

Deep in thought, Jack returned to Australian. What should he do? Once mounted, Jack looked around. Behind the church, the blackened walls of a few European bungalows still smoked. A grey haze lay over the rest of cantonment between him and Sati Chowra Ghat on the river. It was extremely unlikely that his uncle's bungalow was undamaged, and Hari's message had sounded urgent. Swinging around, Jack returned to the entrenchment.

Once Australian was again safely tethered, Jack entered the tiled barracks where General Wheeler and his family had set up quarters in an inner room. He knocked tentatively. The door was opened by a young, immaculately dressed officer. "Yes?"

"I have a message for the general," Jack explained nervously.

"Who is it, Gordon?" and older voice asked from within.

"A boy. Says he has a message for you."

"Send him in. Maybe it's from the relief column."

The officer stood aside and ushered Jack into the room.

General Wheeler, looking old and worn, sat at a desk at one end. At the opposite end, a woman with a noticeably darker skin than the other European women sat preparing a dish of vegetables for cooking. Beside her, Alice Wheeler looked up from her job of cutting a blue dress into long strips.

"Not much of an office," the general observed wryly. "My wife has to prepare food and my daughter, bandages. At least I have my son to act as an aide, and it won't be long before relief arrives."

Jack stole a glance at Gordon Wheeler. He was a tall man, his height accentuated by holding his body rigidly at attention. Jack judged he was about thirty years old, although he wore old-fashioned whiskers down his cheeks and across to join with a full mustache. His sharp features, pale blue eyes and fair skin gave no hint of his mixed heritage. Even in these unmilitary surroundings, Gordon's uniform was perfectly pressed and every button and badge gleamed.

"Now," the general's voice brought Jack's attention back. "What news from the column?"

"I . . . I'm not from the relief column, sir." Jack stammered. Disappointment flickered over the general's face. Jack continued quickly. "I met my aunt's stable boy over by the church. He asked me to tell you—"

"Name?" the general asked peremptorily.

"Jack O'Hara, sir."

"No. The native's name."

"Oh. Hari."

General Wheeler nodded in recognition. "One of Moore's spies. Go on."

"He said that Nana Sahib has looted the treasury and gone to bring the army back from the Delhi road."

As Jack spoke, General Wheeler seemed to slowly collapse in on himself. His body sagged and his eyes watered. It was as if he were aging by the second. Jack had a head full of questions. What did the news mean? What was Hari doing bringing it? But he kept silent, fascinated by the old man's collapse.

Eventually, Gordon Wheeler broke the silence. "We must recall all the men and bring in any stores of powder and shot we can find."

General Wheeler appeared not to hear what was said. "Nana has betrayed me," he said in a quiet, distant voice. "He swore loyalty. My family and I ate at his table. He was my friend."

"Father!" the young officer broke in. "We must act."

With a Herculean effort of will, the old general pulled himself out of his reverie. "Yes. Yes. Of course. See to it, Gordon."

His son saluted smartly and left the room.

"Thank you, young man," Wheeler said as his gaze drifted off into the distance.

Jack headed for the door. He couldn't help looking at Alice. She was sitting with the cut up dress on her lap staring at her father. Her face was stern and hard. Jack hurried into the corridor where he almost fell over his aunt, bustling past with a bowl of steaming water.

"Watch where you're going," she said. "Young Lydia Hillersdon has just had a baby. A beautiful little girl. What a story she will have to tell when she grows up."

Where Soldiers Lie

As Jack watch his aunt hurry away, he couldn't stop a tiny thought worming its way into his mind. "If she grows up."

PART III

The Siege

Day 1: Saturday, June 6

The first shot of the siege was fired at ten thirty in the morning from a nine-pounder cannon, which had been hauled into position to the south west of the entrenchment. The ball bounced off the mud wall, flew over the tiled barracks and crushed the legs of a native servant squatting in the dirt beside the kitchen. The man's screams as his life seeped into the ground around him were soon lost in the general pandemonium as panicked mothers herded children out of the courtyard while bullocks and horses, catching the scent of fear, began straining against their tethers and bellowing and whinnying loudly.

In the trench, soldiers and civilians grabbed the loaded muskets stacked against the parapet and nervously peered over the mud wall. A few fired at the scattered figures gathering around the burned houses or manhandling cannons into position, but most just watched and waited.

All able-bodied men had been recruited to help with the defence. Jack and Tommy had been in the trenches most of the night, watching the city burn and listening to scattered musket fire as the *sepoys*, returning from the Delhi road, rampaged through the European quarter, slaughtering the few remaining sahibs and memsahibs they found cowering there.

A second cannon boomed and Jack watched, fascinated, as a black cannonball bounced over the hard ground and crashed into the parapet to his right.

Gradually, the intensity of the bombardment increased until round shot was flying through the entrenchment from all sides and musket balls whizzed overhead with an annoying whine. The screaming continued and small groups of women and children ran about at random trying to find somewhere safe to hide. Soon, sad piles of clothing stained with blood dotted the open areas. The safest place was in the trench itself, but even there, a careless soldier would expose himself once too often and scream in agony.

"The *sepoys* appear to be back from Delhi," Tommy observed as a musket ball thudded into the breastworks in front of him.

Jack couldn't reply. His mouth was too dry. He huddled as low as he could with his back to the parapet, watching the chaos in the compound and trying not to shake too visibly. His stomach was doing somersaults and he had a strong urge to throw up. Twenty feet away, a cannonball cut a running man in two in a spray of blood. Jack swallowed hard. If he had one wish, it would be to sink into the earth and disappear. He was surprised at how scared he was. Being on his own in the bush had never bothered him. Once he had even faced down a bear that wanted to steal his bag of grouse. Afterward, he had been shaken, but at the time he had acted calmly and coolly with none of the gut-wrenching terror he felt now.

But this was different from being self-sufficient in the wild. Here, other than crouching as low as possible, Jack's fate was entirely out of his hands. Forces much larger than him were at work, and death was being delivered suddenly and randomly all about him.

Oddly, Tommy seemed almost to be enjoying himself. "We disabled all the cannons we couldn't bring into the entrenchment. They must 'ave had others 'idden somewhere. Nana Sahib 'ad a few old brass cannons that the company allowed 'im to keep for ceremonials—that might 'ave been a mistake. What a Turkish, eh?"

"What a what?"

"Turkish baff—laugh. You're slow on the uptake, me ol' china."

"And now we are going to die because of that mistake," Jack said shakily.

"Nah. They're only firing nine and twelve pounders and they're set up too far away. If people would calm down and stay in shelter they would be all right. Look, the cannonballs aren't doing any damage to the barrack walls. It's safe as 'ouses in there, as it is in the trench. Our problems will begin if they bring in 'eavier guns, eighteen or twenty-four pounders, or set up mortars."

"What's a mortar?"

"Same as a cannon, 'cept it fires a shell up in the air. That way the shell can come down behind any fortifications. A well-trained mortar crew could drop a shell through the roof of the barracks as easy as you could flip a pebble into a puddle."

"Will they kill us all?"

"Given enough time, yes. This is not the most defensible position. If it were just filled with soldiers it wouldn't be too bad but there are all the women and nippers.

"But don't you worry," Tommy went on hurriedly once he saw Jack's panicked face. "Our cannon will see off any attack over the open ground and we can 'old out until relief comes from Allahabad."

"How long will that be?"

"A few days, the general says."

"Damn the general," Jack shouted above the din. "How long can we hold out?"

"Three or four weeks, I'd say. Plenty of time for relief to come. If it wasn't for the women and children, this'd be a fine adventure."

"Adventure?" Jack stared at his friend. Tommy's eyes were wide with excitement.

"'Course. This is what I joined up for. There's no adventure in being elbow deep in fish guts behind me dad's shop in London. This is where medals are won."

Jack shook his head in wonder. At this moment, he would give everything he owned to be gutting fish in London.

A shadow passed over Jack as a terrified horse broke loose, leaped the trench and galloped away over the open ground toward the mutineers.

"Australian!" Jack shouted, jumping out of the trench and sprinting through the chaos toward the barracks. He was vaguely aware of Tommy yelling at him to not be a fool.

Australian was standing behind the tiled barracks, his reins tied to a wooden peg that protruded from the mud brick wall. He was stamping his feet, snorting and tossing his head from side to side. His eyes were wide with fear.

"It's all right, boy," Jack said, patting the distraught animal's head. "You'll be fine here."

A round shot crashed into the wall above the pair, showering them with brick dust.

"Sssh." Jack calmed his horse. "I know it's frightening. I'm scared too. Tommy seems to be enjoying himself, but I feel like I'm going to be sick. I'm shaking and I can barely talk."

Jack paused and Australian nuzzled his neck. The horse's breath was warm on his skin and smelled comfortingly of hay.

"But, you know, Australian, I was terrified in the trench, but not now. My stomach has settled and my mouth isn't dry. I think it was the inactivity. I was fine as soon as I came over to see you. Look." Jack held out his hand. It was steady. Australian snuffled it, looking for a treat. "I'm sorry, old boy. I don't have anything. I don't think there will be many treats until the relief column gets here, but Tommy says it will be only a few days and we can hang on until then."

Jack gave Australian a final pat and sprinted over to the tiled-roof barracks to check on his aunt and uncle. He found them in their corner of an inner room. Uncle James looked frightened, wringing his hands and jumping every time a cannonball thudded into the outside wall. Jack wondered why he wasn't in the trenches or helping the artillerymen handle the cannons. Aunt Katherine was the opposite. She sat against the wall, a picture of calm, cradling a bundle of blankets in her arms. As Jack approached, she opened the blankets to show the tiny face of a newborn baby.

"It's the Hillersdon baby," she explained. "Isn't she beautiful?"

Jack said yes, but he thought no. Babies didn't interest him and this one looked as if it was wearing a wrinkled elephant skin two sizes too big.

"Lydia and Charles stepped outside for a minute to discuss names. They need a good strong one for the poor wee mite. These are not good times to be born."

"Hardly proper." Jack couldn't resist the dig. Aunt Katherine seemed remarkably calm in the midst of all the chaos. Perhaps seeing people worse off than herself put things in perspective, or perhaps she felt she had to put on a brave face for her husband. In any case, right now, she was an island of sanity in the middle of madness.

Aunt Katherine smiled. "It doesn't seem important now, does it? In normal circumstances it is, standards must to be maintained. It is how society functions, everyone in their proper place. But the standards have changed. We must all help each other if we are to pull through. After all, the general's family is running the same risk as the postmaster. There will be time enough to make things proper again once this nonsense is all over."

A cannonball thudded into the outer wall and Uncle James shuddered.

"Is Uncle James all right?" Jack asked.

"Oh yes," Aunt Katherine answered for her husband. "He's not really a military type. And I fear he is coming down with a touch of fever."

Jack glanced at his uncle. His skin certainly looked pale and a sheen of sweat was visible on his forehead. Jack was about to ask how he was feeling, when a spine-chilling scream echoed from outside. Jack leaped to his feet and rushed toward the sound.

Jack squeezed past Gordon Wheeler, who was standing in the doorway, into the hot sun. The sight before him made his stomach heave. Lydia Hillersdon stood, her hands over her face, wailing inconsolably. On the ground before her, her husband, Charles, sat against the wall. His face looked calm, but a terrible wound had opened his stomach, exposing glistening entrails.

"Look after the baby," he said and slumped to one side.

"Get her inside," Gordon Wheeler ordered Jack. "I'll get him over to the hospital."

Jack knew there was no point in taking Charles Hillersdon to the hospital, but he said nothing. He took Lydia by the arm and led her in to Aunt Katherine and her newborn daughter.

Day 2: Sunday, June 7

A ll through the night of June 6, the mutineers moved their cannon closer, brought in heavier weapons and mortars, and positioned snipers on the roofs of the surrounding buildings. Jack awoke from his cramped sleep in the trenches to a very different situation from the day before. The nine-pound shot was more frequent and now came from all sides. Eighteen- and twenty-four-pound shot was also added to the barrage and had the force to penetrate the barrack walls, causing chaos and terror inside. On top of it all, the open ground was now swept by musket fire. By midday most of the tents that officers had put up in the compound had been flattened and the abandoned carts and furniture reduced to matchsticks.

"One 'undred and eighty," Tommy said.

"One hundred and eighty what?" Jack asked his friend. Oddly, most of yesterday's fear had dissipated, even though their situation was more dangerous today.

"Cannonballs every hour. I've been timing them on me kettle." Tommy waved his prized watch at Jack as if to prove his point. "There are about three balls arriving in the entrenchment every minute. That's about one 'undred and eighty every hour or, if you prefer, one every twenty seconds."

"I'm glad you're not wasting your time. They can't keep up that rate, can they?"

"Naw, they could probably double it if they worked harder, and it'll slacken at night. Some days'll be worse than others, but there's nuffing we can do to stop them lobbing as many balls in 'ere as they wish."

"Have you also worked out why the *sepoys* haven't attacked us yet? There's three or four thousand of them and only three hundred armed men in here. Surely, they could overwhelm us in a determined charge."

"Possibly, but they would suffer very 'eavily to do it. Our old nine pounders aren't much use at long range, but they're devastating firing grapeshot at cavalry and infantry. We also 'ave mostly Enfield rifled muskets that are much more accurate than the *sepoys*' smoothbore muskets, and we don't mind biting the greased cartridges. Finally, some officers 'ave been putting the word about that we 'ave mined the parade ground in front of the entrenchment and any attack over it will be blown to pieces."

"It's not true, though?"

"No, but would you risk it? So, why should they bovver to attack? They can sit back and shell us to pieces."

"But that will take time."

"Undoubtedly. This is not the best position but we 'ave supplies and ammunition enough for at least a couple of weeks."

"But that's terrible." A frightening thought formed in Jack's head. "If they're not attacking, it means that they are not in a hurry to destroy us. That must mean that the relief column is nowhere near."

Tommy was thoughtfully silent for a moment. "You're beginning to think like a soldier. Yes, the column probably isn't as close as some of us would wish. Still, they will be marching 'ard and it won't be more than a week or so, I'd guess. When the *sepoys* do attack, we'll know they are close."

The pair hunched down, each contemplating the significance of Jack's calculations.

"You know," Jack said at length, "your cockney accent gets stronger when you are excited and almost disappears when you are explaining some obscure military matter. You almost sound like a proper officer sometimes."

"Well, fank you, me ow china." Tommy said with a thick accent. "I only lets it come frew wiv you. Don't wanna be known as the 'Cockney General,' do I? So, I practise alla time when I'm on me ownsome."

"You'd rather be known as the general who talks to himself?"

Tommy laughed. "I've almost got it. In the officer's mess, you would 'ardly know I wasn't the second son from some rural estate in Kent. The only thing I still 'ave trouble with is dropping the aitches, but it'll come, you'll see."

Three cannonballs in quick succession slammed into the hospital barracks.

"If your timing is correct, there'll be a few seconds before more cannonballs come over," Jack said. "I'm going to check on Australian."

"Keep your 'ead down."

In a crouching run, Jack headed for the tiled barracks. The sight that met him as he rounded the corner stopped him cold. Australian lay on his belly, his forelegs folded under him and his long head resting on the ground. A neat, round hole gaped red in the centre of his forehead.

"No!" Jack screamed, lunging forward and throwing his arms around his dead horse's neck. His friend was gone, his island of stability amid the chaos. Who could he tell his secret dreams to now? All the pent-up emotion of the last two days concentrated into a hopeless sense of loss and Jack wept uncontrollably.

When he was empty of tears, Jack heard a soft voice behind him, "Was that your horse?" He turned to see Alice Wheeler watching him.

Jack rubbed his tear-stained face. "Yes. His name was Australian."

"I'm sorry, but I think he may have been lucky."

"Lucky?" Jack felt a seed of anger grow within him. He had just lost the most important thing in the world to him and here was this upper-class girl saying poor Australian was lucky. "He's dead."

"But it looks as if it was quick and painless. There was no shelter for him and he could have been maimed and died in agony. I fear many of us might envy his end before this is over."

Jack's anger turned to puzzlement. "What do you mean?"

"Father has just received word that Colonel Neill's relief force is not at Allahabad. He is only at Benares, more than two hundred miles down river. It will take them longer than everyone thinks to fight their way here."

Jack stared at this beautiful girl who was calmly giving him such devastating news. "No wonder they are not attacking. We don't have enough food for that long. And everyone thinks relief is only a few days away."

"And that is probably just as well. There will be less panic. As to the food situation, that is another reason poor old Australian was lucky."

How did she stay calm under these conditions? Alice should be hysterical and needing comfort and reassurance like nearly all the other women. Yet here she was outlining what might well be the death of them all. Jack's anger flared again. "You're wrong."

Alice answered with an ironic smile. "Just because I am a girl doesn't mean that I don't know things and cannot think. In fact, being a girl is an advantage. Father and the other officers ignore me. They don't think a mere girl can understand the workings of the military mind. I admit that sometimes it confuses me, but I understand more than they think."

"I'm sure your father is doing what is best for us."

"Don't patronize me!" Alice's head snapped up and her eyes blazed. "My father is a doddering old fool. He refused to let us move to a building the soldiers could defend properly. He let cannons, powder and most of the province's treasury fall into the mutineer's hands. He even refused to lay up enough supplies of food for us. All because he put his trust in the man who has now set himself up as lord of the mutineers. My father has killed us all."

She turned on her heel and stalked back to the barracks. A cannonball bounced across the open ground and smashed into the pile of beer and rum barrels the soldiers had so laboriously brought into the entrenchment two days before. A wave of dark alcohol washed out and soaked into the dry ground. Alice ignored it.

Jack watched her go with his mouth open. He was shocked at Alice's forthright speech and her anger at her own father, but mostly he was horrified at the thought that they were all doomed to die.

Day 5: Wednesday, June 10

As evening approached on the fifth day of the siege, Jack was on duty in the trenches, half asleep and pondering their situation. The days had developed a depressing monotony. As measured on Tommy's watch, the rate of shelling had varied, reaching a high of four hundred and fifty cannonballs per hour, and the snipers targeted anyone foolish enough to stand about in the daylight. But nightfall brought a welcome relief from the cannonade and the excruciating heat, allowing some activity.

There had been no major attack, but every day several more defenders succumbed to enemy action—like poor Lydia Hillersdon and her new baby, who were crushed beneath a collapsing wall—or from the effects of heat, fever, or simply giving up hope. Too many on most days to allow burial within the entrenchment. A subsidiary well, outside the defensive wall, had been declared a sepulchre to accommodate the dead. Each day, the dead were tagged and laid out by the hospital wall. Every night, solemn parties carried them out to the well and, as gently as possible, slid the corpses into the depths.

"Here they come!"

Jack sat bolt upright, grabbed his musket and peered over the parapet. Instead of a horde of *sepoys* and cavalry charging across the open ground, he was surprised to see a solitary turbaned horseman. A few musket balls kicked up dust around the figure and the horse was seen to stagger once, before the order to cease fire was given.

Jack ducked as the mysterious horseman leaped the parapet and came to a halt by the barracks. Jack had time only to recognize that the man was a British officer and that what he had taken to be a turban was actually a blood-stained rag before he was hustled in to report to the general.

Almost instantly, rumours swept around the defending soldiers—the man was from the relief column, he was the last survivor of some destroyed station, he was a messenger from Lucknow. Jack discovered the truth only when Tommy joined him after dark.

"It's Lieutenant Boulton of the 7th Native Cavalry. They were on their way to 'elp the missionaries at Fatehgarh when their men mutinied. Lieutenant Boulton was the only officer to escape, although 'e took a musket ball through the cheek. He has had some adventures these last few days."

"So he brings no word from the relief column?"

"No. But I didn't come to bring you the gossip. Captain Moore 'as persuaded the general to allow a party out to disable the closest guns. We are to go tonight."

"We?"

"Of course. I volunteered us both for the adventure. I knew you wouldn't want to miss it."

"Thanks very much." Jack peered uncertainly over the parapet. "Those guns are a long way off."

"Stop groaning. Do you want to sit 'ere and be a target forever? This is a chance to 'it back. To show the mutineers that we 'ave some fight in us. Perhaps they will think twice before moving their cannons up close when they see we 'ave some sting left. You must come."

"All right," Jack agreed, swayed by his friend's enthusiasm. Inadequate as the entrenchment's defences were, Jack was loathe to leave them. He would feel almost naked out there on the open plain, and the thought of getting into close combat with a fanatical *sepoy* wielding a cold bayonet made him shudder. But Jack couldn't let his friend down, and, maybe, this exploit would impress Alice.

The pair joined a group of about twenty men huddled beside the hospital barracks. Jack recognized several as officers, but they all wore various articles of drab clothing instead of their red jackets. They were also busily smearing their faces with lamp black and ashes.

"This is to be a lightening raid," Moore instructed. "No heroics. If I am correct, we will catch the gunners napping. We bayonet whomever we find, disable the guns and haul off anything we can. Stick together. Let's go."

Moving in a single file, the party crossed the trench, worked its way along the line of unfinished buildings, across a deep drainage ditch and toward the native infantry barracks. Jack's heart pounded and his hands sweated uncontrollably. Every shadow seemed to contain a mutineer ready to leap out and slash at him with his sword. The only thing that kept him going was the presence of Tommy and the other men. Without them, he would have fled back to the entrenchment. He wondered if the others felt the same. Perhaps none of them could do this on his own.

At the front of the line, Moore held up his hand as a signal for them to stop. Silently, the men arranged themselves in a line facing the mutineer's battery. Dark shapes moved between the guns. Despite Captain Moore's hunch, the enemy hadn't been caught napping. Part of Jack was disappointed that the surprise hadn't worked. The other part was relieved; now, they'd have to go back to the relative safety of the entrenchment. But Jack had underestimated the captain. Communicating only through hand signals passed from one man to the next, the line raised their primed muskets and a deafening volley crashed out. Then all hell broke loose.

"Come on!" Moore yelled as he led the men between the guns. "Spike the nine pounders!"

All around, men were hammering spikes into the fuse holes of the cannons, rendering them useless. Others were bayoneting the gunners who had been wounded in the volley. In the darkness around them, voices shouted and musket shots cracked, but nothing was aimed and the balls flew harmlessly overhead.

"All right," Moore shouted above the din, "Let's get back before they organize themselves."

Loaded with the dead gunners' muskets and as much powder and shot as they could carry, the party staggered across the open ground toward the entrenchment. All around them, the musket fire was becoming heavier and more accurate and an occasional cannonball bounced over the dry earth.

Where Soldiers Lie

They were about twenty yards from the mud wall when Jack was kicked in the back. At least, that's what it felt like—the time Australian had kicked Jack. Confused, he fell heavily forward into the dust. How could Australian be here? He was dead, wasn't he? But if not Australian, then whom? Who had kicked him? And why did his back feel so oddly numb? Through the fog in his mind, Jack felt hands reach under his arms.

"Come on, let's get you inside." Jack found he could move his legs and began to help.

"That's it," Tommy said. "Don't leave all the work to me."

By the time he was half dragged into the hospital, Jack had come to a startling realization: he had been shot. He was dumped unceremoniously on a pile of straw while the doctor cut a hole in his shirt. Jack could feel the man working on his back, but there was no pain. Eventually, he heard a sigh.

"You're a very lucky young man" A hand reached around and showed him a round, lead musket ball. "It was almost spent. Only had enough power to break the skin, but if it had penetrated deeply, you would be dead now for sure. If it doesn't become infected, you'll just have a nice neat scar to show your grandchildren. Just let me put a bandage on it."

The doctor reached for a strip of cloth and began winding it around Jack's shoulder. Jack noticed that it was a strip of blue dress material. He wondered if it was Alice Wheeler's. "How's the wounded hero?" Jack rolled onto his side to see Alice standing nearby holding a basin of water.

"Hardly a hero," Jack said. "I'm afraid I'm not even a very good soldier. I was shot in the back while retreating and I didn't even fire my musket."

"It's not such a bad thing not to have tried to kill someone, and there's nothing wrong with being scared."

"I wasn't scared," Jack said, indignantly.

"Of course not," Alice said, a smile flickering across her face. She turned to go.

Jack cursed himself for his outburst. Now she was going to leave, and all he really wanted was to keep her talking. "That's not true."

Alice looked back at him.

"I was terrified. I thought I was going to die. I wish I *was* brave, like Captain Moore."

"To be truly brave, you have to be scared first. It's overcoming the fear that's the challenge. And fear is a sign of intelligence. You need imagination to be scared. Crocodiles don't feel fear."

"Crocodiles have nothing to be frightened of."

"You've never been on a crocodile hunt then—seen them driven into shallow water and shot. Unless the marksman is very good it can take a long time to kill a large crocodile. But they keep fighting to the last. It's just instinct, though. Crocodiles are stupid."

"Stupid? They terrify me. I hate the thought of being dragged alive into their lair."

"They're nothing to be scared of. Do you know the story of the crocodile and the monkey?"

"No," Jack said. He was delighted to see Alice crouch comfortably beside him.

"Once, long ago, a crocodile and his wife lived in the River Ganges—up near the mountains where it is forested. Every day, the crocodile's wife watched a huge monkey swing through the trees. In time, she developed an overwhelming desire to eat the monkey's heart, so she went to her husband and asked him to get it for her.

"The crocodile agreed and made a plan. He went up to the monkey while he was drinking and said, 'Dearest monkey, I see you have eaten the best fruit on this side of the river. There are wonderful mango and fig trees on the other side.'

"'I know,' the monkey replied, 'but I cannot swim.'

"'I will take you over on my back,' the crocodile offered.

"'Very well,' the monkey agreed, trustingly, and climbed on the crocodile's back.

"Half way over, the crocodile began to sink.

"'Good friend,' said the monkey. 'Why are you letting me sink?'

"'Because I wish to drown you and take your heart back as a present for my lovely wife.'

"'I must tell you,' said the monkey, thinking quickly, 'we monkeys do not carry our hearts with us all the time. If we did, they would get bruised as we leaped from tree to tree.'

"The crocodile had seen the monkey leaping about the trees and, since he lived in the river and could imagine nothing else, this seemed to make sense to him. 'Where do you keep it?'

"'In the large fig tree over there. It is hanging from a high branch.'

"'I cannot see it,' the crocodile complained.

"'Take me over there and I shall point it out to you.'

"So the crocodile swam to the bank. As soon as he reached it the monkey leaped off his back and climbed the fig tree, where he sat singing, 'Great is your body, truly, but how much smaller is your wit! Now go away, sir crocodile, for I have had the best of it.'

"So, you see," Alice said with a smile. "Crocodiles are stupid and you are smart. If a monkey can outwit one, surely you can too."

Jack decided not to point out that crocodiles can't talk. "How do you know that story?"

"I read it," she said, standing up.

"Read it? Where?"

"Oh, it's a common story, and the Hindi is quite simple. Now get some rest, brave soldier."

Jack watched Alice go with something approaching awe. Not only was she beautiful, outspoken and easy to talk to, she could also read Hindi. Suddenly, Jack saw at least one benefit in a longer siege. As long as they were trapped in the entrenchment he would be close to Alice, and the social barriers that would normally prevent them from talking could be ignored. A wave of guilt swept over him—how could he even think about benefiting from such tragic events—but he drifted off to sleep, nonetheless, a half-smile on his lips.

Day 8: Saturday, June 13

Jack watched disinterestedly as the ragged figure began its hunched, stumbling run to the well. As opposed to the sepulchral well, which lay some distance outside the entrenchment, the working well, the garrison's only supply of water, lay in the open area between the two barrack buildings. Jack thought it odd that two wells were used for such different purposes: one as a grave, the other as an essential to life. What they had in common was that neither could be safely visited in daylight. The man must be crazed by the heat and thirst to attempt such a suicidal journey. The rebel snipers were not good shots but there were a lot of them and, when they spotted a figure in the open, the hail of musket balls often found its mark. On top of that, the cannons used the well as a convenient aiming point.

The man had reached the well and was now engaged in the most dangerous part of his quest. Although the raised walls provided some protection, the laborious process of lowering the bucket and then hauling it back up—the pulley mechanism had long since disintegrated—meant that he would have to remain in the same spot, a stationary target, for a long time.

Jack thought of the cool water lying sixty feet down the well. It was noon, but already his mouth was parched. What little water was left in his canteen tasted strongly metallic and was almost too hot to drink. Jack would sell his soul to the devil for a long, cool drink of water—or a swim in the pool below the falls near where he and his parents had lived. He would dive in and just let the water soak into his dehydrated, sun-blistered body. He could almost feel the glorious coolness wrapping around him, driving back the hideous burden of heat.

"A rupee says 'e don't make it back," Tommy croaked through cracked lips.

Jack turned his aching head to look at his friend. Both were lying in the trench behind what was left of the mud wall. They were there to guard against a surprise attack, but it was the safest place to be and the shallow depression also contained a few women and children who were willing to forego the shade of the barracks for the cruel heat of the open sun.

Early in the siege, the barracks had appeared to be the safest place, but appearances had proved illusory. The brick walls would stop a musket ball or a nine-pounder shot, but the heavy eighteen- and twenty-four-pound shot went through them like a hot knife through butter. Both buildings were now honeycombed with holes. Some people found that the strain of waiting for sudden death to crash through a wall a few feet away was far worse than enduring the heat in the open.

"All right, you're on," Jack agreed, thinking that if he won, he might even risk a sprint across the open to see if he could buy a cup of the cool water from the man. A part of Jack's tired mind wondered how, in only a week, they could have sunk low enough to be betting on a man's life, but what difference did it make? The man would live or die regardless of what Jack and Tommy did.

The man had already hauled the bucket up and was now beginning his slow journey back to the barracks. He proceeded as carefully as he could, but water still splashed out onto the dust where occasional musket balls kicked up tiny clouds. Jack found he couldn't take his eyes off the bucket. He gasped with disappointment each time a wave splashed out and was lost.

The man was three-quarters of the way back to the hospital barracks when the cannonball found him. It was a random shot—no one aimed an eighteen-pound cannon at a single man—but it was accurate. Jack saw the ball bounce once before it hit the bucket. Water sprayed like a tiny monsoon, the bucket—suddenly an unrecognizable lump of tin—flew through the air, and the blow hurled the man to one side.

In an instant, the man was back on his feet, but instead of running for cover, he threw himself at the damp patch of ground, which was already steaming in the heat. After scrabbling in the dirt for his lost treasure, he rose and made a slow dispirited retreat to the barracks.

"I win!" Tommy exclaimed.

"No you don't," Jack argued. "He made it back safely."

"But 'e lost the water."

"Doesn't matter, the man was the bet."

"You wouldn't last five minutes in the regimental barracks," Tommy said as he reluctantly searched his pockets for a rupee. "Don't spend it rashly."

"I think I'll buy a block of ice—a big one like the ones they put in the carriages of the trains to cool them down—lie back, sit it on my chest and let it melt over me."

"It'd crush you."

"But what a way to go." Jack squinted up at the washed out sky. The sun was as much an enemy as the mutinous *sepoys*. It almost seemed to have a malevolent character all its own—dehydrating bodies, blackening and blistering exposed skin and pushing fevered minds into gibbering insanity. Nearly unbearable heat was radiating at Jack from all directions. It was as if he were under a pale blue dome that was being relentlessly heated on the outside. "It would be better than being baked to death."

"True enough, but I think the cannonballs will get us first." Tommy paused reflectively. "Captain Wyndham caught it this morning, over by the redoubt. A twenty-four-pounder ball right in the chest. Wasn't much left. I think that's what 'e wanted."

"Wanted?"

"Yes. He had been wandering around in the open a lot these past days—ever since his two little girls were killed. I think 'e kept going as long as 'e did for his missus, but she lost 'eart, wouldn't talk to anyone and woke up at all ours of the night screaming for her kids. She died yesterday."

Every day the death toll rose through enemy fire, sickness and heat, and every night the burial party carted the bodies out to the sepulchral well. There were almost a hundred in there already.

"Where do you think the relief force is?" Jack asked, raising the main topic of conversation in the entrenchment. "Colonel Neill must be close by now. He was in Benares on June 4. Two weeks hard marching is ample time to get here. And perhaps Lawrence will send us help from Lucknow. The general sent a messenger out asking for aid."

"I doubt if Lawrence can do anything. He'll be having his own difficulties—only one regiment of loyal troops and almost a thousand women, children and civilians to look after."

Jack felt a wave of anger at Tommy's negativity, but he was too tired to express it.

Tommy went on. "If it weren't for the women and children, we could fight our way through to Lucknow or the relieving column, but not with 'undreds of noncombatants in tow.

"'Ow are your aunt and uncle 'olding out?"

A cannonball demolished part of the outer verandah of the hospital barracks in a cloud of dust and flying wood splinters. Only a few days ago, this would have caused a panic with women and children screaming and men rushing to help the injured. Now, apart from a minor commotion among those who were sheltering close by, it was met with apathy. Destruction had become too common.

"Oddly," Jack said, licking his lips, "Aunt Katherine is faring better. She was always so wrapped up in doing things the proper way—worrying about appearances—that I assumed she would collapse when something serious happened. But she is an entirely different person. She has ripped her precious dresses up to make bandages and spends every waking hour in the hospital helping the doctors care for the wounded. It's Uncle James who has fallen apart."

"But your uncle was wounded, wasn't 'e?"

"A spent musket ball grazed his cheek. It was nothing. True, he has a fever, but there are many with much worse. He just lies in the hospital. I know he's not a soldier, but a lot of the civilians are helping out, learning to man the cannons and such."

"It is odd. I've seen it many times in battle. The one you think is the bravest turns and runs while the quiet, unassuming one performs the 'eroics. I think it's because—"

Tommy was interrupted by a loud hiss as a smoking bomb soared overhead and crashed into the thatched roof of the hospital barracks. The missile bounced twice before splitting open and pouring burning fuel everywhere. In seconds the tinder-dry thatch was ablaze and black smoke was filling the building. Screaming women and children burst from doors and windows completely heedless of the musket and cannon fire sweeping the open ground.

Jack leaped to his feet. "We've got to get the wounded out." Before he could take a step, Tommy grabbed him by the shoulders and pulled him back down.

"No! We 'ave to stay 'ere. As soon as the *sepoys* see the fire, they'll attack, assuming we've all gone to 'elp."

As if in response to Tommy's statement, the rate of cannon fire increased. In front of Jack, a woman collapsed in the dust.

"We have to help them," Jack yelled, struggling to break free from his friend's grip.

"We will, by staying 'ere. Look."

Tommy hauled Jack around. Across the open ground, hundreds of figures were rising from trenches and racing out from behind walls. Most were still dressed in the remnants of British army uniforms, but many wore traditional native dress. Some paused to fire muskets while others rushed forward, brandishing ugly, curved swords—*tulwars* Jack remembered vaguely—that glinted in the sunlight.

It looked terrifying, but Tommy had taught Jack enough for him to recognize that the attack was ill-prepared and badly coordinated. The men were running in a loose mass, with no coherent leadership and they were not supported by a cavalry charge. Several rounds of grapeshot and volleys of musket fire left dozens of bloody heaps on the ground and sent the remainder scurrying back for shelter.

"Now we can go and 'elp," Tommy said grimly.

The pair rushed across the open ground to the barracks. Although one end of the hospital was an inferno, it was still possible to enter the other. Without a second thought, Jack dashed in. The scene that met him through the thickening smoke was horrific. Those who could were dragging themselves toward the door. Those too sick or badly wounded to move lay where they were, screaming for help.

The smoke stung Jack's eyes and caught harshly in his throat. Fighting back the urge to flee, he grabbed a soldier with heavily bandaged legs and began dragging him toward the door.

The man's neighbour, his head swathed in a blood-stained piece of frilly underskirt, waved his arm blindly. "Bill? What's happening. Don't leave me, Bill. I can't see and I don't have the strength to stand. Help me!"

"I'll come back and get you," Jack said.

Bill screamed every time his useless legs flopped against a bump on the interminable journey to the door, but Jack ignored him. Finally they made it clear of the building into the fresh air where Jack collapsed retching. By the time he recovered enough to turn back to the building, thick smoke was already billowing out the door and the screams from inside were fading. Nevertheless, he headed back in to help the blind soldier.

He was at the threshold, when he was bowled over by the hacking, smoke-blackened figure of a woman clutching a child to her chest. The woman put the child down and sat coughing beside Jack. She was filthy, her hair wild and the hem of her dress scorched and smouldering.

"Aunt Katherine?"

The woman raised a smudged face. The tear stains were not all from the smoke. "Those poor children," she wheezed.

"I'll get more." Jack started toward the door.

His aunt's thin hand held him back. "No! It's impossible."

As if emphasizing her words, a large section of roof collapsed with a roar, sending bright flames licking out the door. When the sound died, the screaming stopped.

"Must be twenty or thirty still in there." Jack looked at his aunt. She sat in a huddle, gazing up at him. She was so different from the woman he remembered sweeping through the bungalow, organizing the servants and trying to arrange the world in the proper way, that he had trouble believing she was the same person. She spoke distractedly, as much to herself as to Jack. "I don't think James made it. He was so weak with the fever and he was too heavy for me. I could carry only a child."

"Uncle James?"

Aunt Katherine nodded weakly. "It's for the best. He had given up, you know, and we must never do that. However difficult it gets, never give up." The old lady's gaze wandered over the desolation of the entrenchment but Jack had the strong feeling that she wasn't seeing any of it. "I think it was a mistake for James to bring us out here all those years ago. He thought we would get on better, but he never really adjusted to the heat or the people. It was all too different. Perhaps if we had had children?"

With a visible effort, Aunt Katherine pulled herself back from the past. "But there are things to be done. These poor mites need us. Help me get them and the wounded into the shelter of the other barracks."

All afternoon, Jack worked in the blazing sun, carrying the sick and wounded survivors of the fire into the shade of the remaining barracks. Many times he was convinced there was no space left in the shade but some was always created, sometimes by the death of a person Jack had to haul out into the sun to await a final nighttime journey to the sepulchral well. One of the bodies belonged to the soldier with the injured legs.

Often, Jack thought of collapsing somewhere, but the sight of his aunt, toiling tirelessly with the children, forced him to continue. Eventually, however, he could take no more and sat as close as he could to the still smouldering hospital barracks. He had just drained the last of the disgusting liquid from his water bottle when he heard a voice.

"Until now, I don't think I could have believed a week could be so long." The filthy figure of Alice slumped down beside Jack. He had seen her occasionally during the afternoon, but had been too busy and tired to give her much thought.

"It won't be much longer, now," he said, parroting the comforting words that everyone said and few believed.

"Until what?" Alice challenged him.

"The relief column arrives."

"Colonel Neill's relief column?" She glanced up at the makeshift crow's nest atop the barracks, where there was always a figure braving shot and musket fire to keep a watch on the Allahabad road. "Don't hold your breath."

"What do you mean?"

Alice turned her gaze on Jack. "Colonel Neill is at Allahabad with the 1st Madras Fusiliers, waiting for General Havelock to join him from Calcutta. By all accounts, he is more concerned with hanging rebels by the roadside than pushing on to relieve us."

"That can't be true. He was in Benares ten days ago. He should be almost here by now."

Alice shrugged. "Should is not the same as is. A spy came into the entrenchment last night with the news. Neill and Havelock can't be here for two weeks at the earliest."

"The garrison at Lucknow will come to our aid."

"They are not in much better shape than we are. They will need every man they have there to defend the residency when their *sepoys* mutiny. At least they are well-prepared."

"Can we hold out long enough?"

"We have no choice. The spy also told us something that happened yesterday. Some 120 men, women and children from Fatehgarh were murdered less than a mile from here."

"What?" Jack's tired brain was having trouble understanding what Alice was telling him.

"They were coming down the river to escape from the mutiny there. They ran aground on a sandbar and were captured. Yesterday afternoon, Nana Sahib had them slaughtered. The spy saw it all."

Jack sat in stunned silence. It was one thing to risk death in a siege or battle, but to be massacred in cold blood?

"So, you see, we must keep going."

"It must be a mistake."

"It's no mistake. The spy saw it all as he was waiting for dark to slip into the entrenchment."

"Can we hold out long enough?"

Alice shrugged. "Father doesn't think so. He is very low—hard on himself for not preparing better—but some of the younger officers, Captain Moore mainly, are convinced we can if we just don't give up hope. I think we can."

Jack stared at the incredibly confident girl in front of him. "How do you keep your hope up?"

"I have spent my life in hope." Alice smiled and her white teeth flashed against the grime of her face. "As I told you at the Bibighar before this madness began, I am a quarter Indian. You are a half. We can never be fully accepted by either culture. It was different in my mother's day, but society is much more rigid now."

"But you are the daughter of a famous general. Tommy says you are popular at the dances."

Alice laughed. "Yes, my dance card is always full, but that is just because I have a pretty face. It means nothing. And the young officers who pay me court are empty-headed; they can talk of nothing but war and battles. It is the older people who have the power in this country. And it's true, being a general's daughter gives me a higher social standing with the people who matter. It forces them to talk to me at parties but it doesn't mean they want to. I hear the sly asides about a 'touch of the tar brush' and see the sideways glances.

"I used to hope it was just my imagination—that it would all go away and everything would be fine. But it won't. Now I simply hope that people will leave me alone to live my own life. And that is where I am lucky being a woman. If I find someone who loves me and doesn't care, he will protect me from all the unpleasantness. I will be quite content to disappear into the background and pursue my own interests. We live in a fascinating time and I look forward to seeing where we go from here. It's more difficult for my brother."

"Gordon, but he doesn't look . . . " Jack stopped as he realized what he had been about to say.

"Half-caste?" Alice finished for him. "You see how pervasive it all is? Gordon *is* pale, and he tries very hard to live in the European world. The army is his life. He thinks that if he is the perfect soldier, he will be accepted. And that may be true, but only in the army. Gordon is thirty-two but he's not married—why?"

"He hasn't found the right woman?"

"There are plenty of 'right women' for a handsome young army officer. Gordon is not married because of the mothers. His skin is the right colour, but everyone knows how 'a touch of the tar brush' can skip a generation. No one wants their daughter to bear half-caste children. So, whenever he shows an interest in a girl, she is suddenly spirited away to the hills or to visit a relative back in England."

"That's terrible," Jack said, wondering if that is what would happen to Alice if he ever openly showed an interest in her.

"It is, but it's the way things are. It'll be even harder for you."

"What do you mean?" Jack asked.

"I don't know if you have looked in a mirror lately, but you are noticeably darker than I am. Especially after being in the open sun for a week. Put on a *dhoti* and a *pagri* and you could pass for a native. It's not a problem now—they still regard you as a child—but see what happens in a few years. You won't be invited to the parties, your application to join the local club will be turned down, the girl *you* fall in love with will suddenly leave town. No one will say it is because your skin's too dark, but that's what it will be."

Jack frowned. He had been so wrapped up in the moment that he hadn't considered his future in detail. It didn't look bright as a part of the ruling class in India, but then he didn't want to be part of that anyway. Maybe he would return to Canada West.

Jack was surprised to find that the idea of going back didn't excite him. Canada West had been his childhood and he wasn't a child any more. He couldn't go back. Besides, in some slow, subtle way, like water seeping through dry mud, India had wormed its way under his skin.

"I love this country," he said, realizing it himself for the first time.

Alice laughed again, a bright, tinkling sound against the backdrop of cannon fire. "That's good, because right now it seems to be doing its best to kill us." Alice's face became serious. "But what are your dreams?"

The question took Jack by surprise. "I want to discover a lost city," he blurted.

"Archaeology. You want to follow Belzoni and Burckhardt to Thebes and Petra—be a fellow 'traveller from an antique land.'"

"I don't want to follow anyone. I'll discover my own city, maybe Troy or Carthage."

"Or one here in India?"

"Perhaps. I've read Seely's discovery of Elora; it's temples."

"But the temples were in cities. They have survived since they were all that was built of stone. The houses were wood or mud and there's nothing left of them. But there are other stone and brick cities."

"Where? I've never heard of any."

"You've never read the ancient books—the Vedas?"

Jack remembered the story Hari had told him. It had been part of the Vedas. "But they're not written in English. Besides, they're just stories."

"Homer wrote stories, yet you will happily rush off and search for Troy."

Jack couldn't argue against that point. He decided to change the topic. "Can you read these ancient books as well as stories of monkeys and crocodiles?"

"A little; they are written in Sanskrit, which is different from Hindi, but some have been translated. They tell of the first invaders, led by the god Indra, coming to India and discovering the Dasas with stone cities and iron forts.

Indra the Vritra-slayer, Fort-destroyer,
scattered the Dasa hosts who dwelt in darkness ...
To him in might the Gods have ever yielded,
to Indra in the tumult of battle.
When in his arms they laid the bolt,
he slaughtered the Dasas
and cast down their forts of iron.

"That was probably around the time the Greeks and Trojans were killing each other."

"Forts of iron?" Jack asked.

"Possibly. Certainly something other than wood. The cities of the Dasas were different enough that the ancient writers remarked on it."

"Where are they?"

"That's the trick," Alice said with a smile. "I've heard stories from soldiers about mysterious mounds in the country along the Indus River and of strange clay seals with unusual designs on them. Maybe that's where to look.

John Wilson

"It's good to have dreams. Let us hope we all live to fulfill them."

Jack watched as Alice rose and made her way back to the tiled barracks. He felt a pang of regret that he had met her under such desperate circumstances. But then again, without these circumstances he would probably never have met her at all. Life was too complicated. Tiredly, Jack headed back to his post in the trenches. Things were simpler there.

Day 9: Sunday, June 14

O ur goal this time is that twenty-four pounder over by St. John's Church." Captain Moore talked as he applied lamp black to his face. "The rules are the same as on previous raids: be fast and stick together. This is our biggest raid so far, so the rules are more important than ever.

"Besides," a smile flashed over Moore's blackened face, "who would want to miss a breakfast of lentils and chapattis?"

A groan rumbled through the group at the mention of their dwindling diet. Jack looked around at the fifty men in the party. They were the fittest left in the entrenchment and yet the faces were all thinner and showing more signs of strain than on the previous raid. Those not killed outright by the heat or the shelling were being steadily worn down—while Neill dallied at Allahabad.

A wave of anger flooded over Jack and he kicked the ground in frustration.

"Easy," Tommy advised. "Save your anger for the raid."

"I've got enough anger for everyone," Jack spat as he stalked away from the group. He didn't want to talk to anyone. He just wanted to go on the raid and get it over with. Fighting was easy and simple; it was dealing with people that was hard.

What was going on? These days Jack's emotions seemed to have a life of their own, swinging wildly from one extreme to the other for no good reason. Was it tension, lack of sleep or some strange illness? Was it the siege? Jack had seen so many helpless women and children die, torn apart by cannonballs or wasted from fever and sickness, it had to affect him. Suddenly, his anger was overwhelmed by pity. He felt on the verge of tears.

Jack took a deep breath and turned away, trying to haul his emotions under control. A figure appeared around the corner of the barrack block. At first, Jack thought it was another volunteer for the raid, arriving late with his face already blackened, but the nod of the head was familiar.

"Hari! What are you doing here?"

"Hello, Jack Sahib. I am most happy to be bumping into you again."

"Why are you in the entrenchment?"

"I am taking note to Lawrence Sahib in Lucknow."

"Was it you who brought in the news of the murder of the Fatehgarh fugitives"

"Sadly, it was so. But please excuse. I must be talking with Moore Sahib."

Hari nodded once more and slipped past, leaving Jack staring into the darkness.

"Hari is one of our most important sources of information," a soft voice beside him made Jack start.

"Alice," he said, without thinking that it was not the

proper way to address the general's daughter.

"Hari also brought the news of Colonel Neill dallying at Allahabad. He can move about Cawnpore with ease and slips in and out of the entrenchment whenever he wants."

"I thought he was nothing more than my aunt's stable boy. He used to look after my horse, Australian."

"A good cover, no?"

"Yes. I suppose so. How many spies does Captain Moore have?"

"A few. Some have been caught and killed or had their hands cut off and tongues cut out, but several still bring us news and take messages out."

"Why is Hari here tonight?"

"He is going out with you. He'll slip away as soon as you are clear of the wall. He has a letter for the garrison at Lucknow."

"Asking for aid."

"Begging for it." Alice hesitated, her face a pale oval in the moonlight. Then she recited: "'We have been besieged since the sixth. Our defence has been noble and wonderful, our loss heavy and cruel. We want aid, aid, aid!'"

"Your father wrote that?"

"He is becoming desperate."

"But we must—"

"Let's go!" Moore's authoritative voice echoed out of the darkness.

"I have to go," Jack said.

Alice nodded. By the time she said, "Be careful," Jack was too far away to hear.

Moore led the way out of the barracks and into the drainage ditch that headed out toward the church. At the road, they turned along a culvert and soon were lying along the base of the stone wall around the churchyard. Jack had seen Hari, a ghostly shape in front of him, but somewhere along the way he had disappeared into the surrounding blackness. Jack silently wished him good luck.

With muskets poised, Moore's men leaped the wall into the graveyard. Incredibly, it was deserted. In response to whispered commands, they spiked two small guns and raced on toward the twenty-four pounder.

The large gun was surrounded by a low wall and was defended by a squad of *sepoy* gunners. Pausing only long enough to fire a volley at the gunners, Moore's squad leaped the wall.

Tommy and Jack went in together and Jack's first sight of close combat stopped him in his tracks. Dark shapes spun and twisted in the flickering light of the gunners' fires. Several pairs of figures were locked in struggles to the death.

As he looked around in stunned inaction, Jack saw Captain Moore engaged with a large *sepoy*. The man had Moore on the ground and was preparing to slit his throat. Jack raised his musket before he realized he had not reloaded after the volley. He was debating what to do when Tommy leaped past him and, with an animal yell, drove his bayonet onto the *sepoy*'s side. The man dropped his knife and flopped over. As Tommy withdrew his weapon, Moore regained his feet, nodded thanks to Tommy and headed for the cannon.

As quickly as it had begun, the fight was over. Half a dozen dark shapes lay lifeless in the dirt and the rest of the gunners fled.

"I'm sorry," Jack said, feeling guilty about his indecision when Moore was attacked.

"Don't worry," Tommy replied. "'And-to-'ands the worst kind of fighting. You'll get used to it."

Jack nodded, but he doubted he would ever get used to it. Tommy had looked into the *sepoy*'s eyes as he had driven the bayonet home. Could Jack kill at such personal range? He didn't think so. At the moment, he didn't have to worry about it. The raiding party was busy destroying the gun. They rammed a misshapen lump of metal into the muzzle, Moore lit a taper at the powder hole and, with a huge roar, the gun split apart. Almost immediately, wild musket fire opened up from all sides.

"Time to go," Moore yelled and the men ran out into the open toward the entrenchment.

Jack ran as hard as he could, the scabbed wound in his back itching annoyingly. Halfway back, the man in front of him staggered and fell. Jack knelt by him as a large pool of dark blood spread out from his head.

"'E's dead," Tommy was beside Jack, a wounded man draped over his back. "We can do nuffing for 'im. Give me an 'and with this one; 'e's taken a ball in the leg."

Carrying the wounded man between them, Jack and Tommy reached the mud wall and tumbled thankfully into the trench. Only taking a moment to draw breath, they continued over to the barrack wall. Jack's aunt met them.

"Set him down here," she said, indicating a space along the wall. "He's the fourth wounded man from the raid. The doctor will get to him as soon as he can, although he won't be able to do much. All the medical instruments went up in the hospital fire. Are you boys all right?"

Jack and Tommy both nodded.

Aunt Katherine stood gazing at Jack for a long moment. Jack lowered his eyes, thinking he was going to get a lecture for going on the raid.

"You're a brave boy," Aunt Katherine said at length. Jack looked up in surprise. "I'm very proud of you. And I think your parents would be, too."

"I . . . ," Jack mumbled, swamped by embarrassment.

His aunt gave him no time to think. "Now go inside and get a drink of water and try to rest. I'll look after this man until the doctor gets to him."

Obediently, the pair went inside. No one was asleep. Everyone had been sitting in terrified silence while the raid was going on, but now they were patting the men on the back and welcoming back loved ones.

"Did Hari get away all right?" Alice appeared beside Jack.

"Yes, I think so. How long has he been working for Captain Moore?"

"Several years. Apparently, Moore ran some sort of spy school before the mutiny. Likely candidates were sent to school and then given some training before they were dispatched all over the country to wait for a job. The Company pays for the boys' education and then uses them for whatever the need is."

"Spying?"

"Yes, but not just that. I'm told me that many are used up on the frontier to map neighbouring countries that might not be friendly to an official surveying team. They are taught to walk so that each step is an exact length, then they dress as *fakirs* or merchants and walk about the country, counting their steps as they walk and turning the information into maps."

"Why?"

"So that the army will have some idea of what is facing them if they ever have to go there."

"So we can invade these countries?"

"Not necessarily. The Company, and the government, are afraid of the Russians. They are expanding their empire toward India and would like nothing more than to control the mountain passes so they could threaten an invasion."

"And Hari is a part of all this?"

"A small part. After school in Lucknow, he came to Cawnpore to wait for an assignment."

"I find it hard to believe that my aunt's stable boy is a spy."

Alice smiled. "This is a complex land. Very little is as it seems."

"At least the raid went well."

Alice's smile faded. "Yes, but it will be the last one. Father has forbidden another."

"He's a fool." The words burst out of Jack before he could stop them.

"I don't think so in this case," Alice said, calmly. "We lost five men—one killed and four wounded—men we no longer have to occupy the trenches. The raids *are* good for morale, but they cost us more than they cost the mutineers. And the men are getting weaker every day. We've been lucky so far, but sooner or later, one of Captain Moore's raids will go wrong. We can't afford to lose ten or a dozen of our fittest defenders."

"I'm sorry. I didn't mean to call your father a fool. I didn't think about the raids that way."

Alice's smile returned. "I told you this was a complex land."

Day 13: Thursday, June 18

The musket leaning against the wall beside Jack suddenly fired a ball straight up into the air. Startled, Jack rolled away from it.

"It's just the 'eat," Tommy explained. "Must be 120 degrees or more today. That's enough to set off the powder charge. I've seen musket stocks so 'ot they blistered men's 'ands when they lifted them to fire."

"Shut up!" Jack shouted, irrational anger at his friend sweeping over him. "I'm sick of hearing your little pieces of information about a soldier's life and experiences. You chose to join the army and go and fight but most of us in here didn't. We didn't ask for this. I don't want to kill anyone and I don't want to die. If Neill's not coming, why don't the *sepoys* attack and get it over with?"

Exhausted by his tirade, Jack slumped back against the wall. He was ashamed. He knew his words were unfair, but he couldn't help himself. Fortunately, Tommy showed no sign that he was upset by his friend's outburst.

Across the open ground, a twenty-four-pound cannonball crashed through the end wall of what was left of the tiled-roof barracks. It probably killed someone inside, but it provoked no response.

Jack watched the dust settle disinterestedly. His anger had left as abruptly as it had arrived. Now he just felt drained. It was as if the heat was a physical presence, weighing down on everyone, too heavy to allow movement or even thought. The only living things moving in the entrenchment were the flies, which congregated in black swarms over the dead bodies awaiting their final journey to the sepulchral well.

"How many are dead now?" Jack groaned, as much to himself as to Tommy.

"Must be near three 'undred," Tommy replied. "Three 'undred dead in near two weeks. It'll take them another month at this rate. Still, I expect we'll run out of food and ammunition before that."

"I wish it would rain." Jack squinted up at the pale, cloudless sky.

"That'd do it. One good rainstorm and our defences will vanish. Then they'll just walk in."

Jack and Tommy sat in the blackened ruins of the hospital barracks. It was a roofless shell, so there was little shade when the sun beat down vertically in the middle of the day. However, since the fire, the *sepoy* gunners had been concentrating on the tiled-roof barracks and this had become one of the safest places in the entrenchment.

"You know what the worst thing is?" Jack asked.

"What?"

"The boredom. I used to think I was bored listening to Aunt Katherine and Uncle James talking about who was

letting the side down by drinking too much at dinner parties—I had no idea. Now I wish hundreds of *sepoys* would
attack and try to kill me just for something to do."

"We might not be able to drive them off."

"At least it would be a quick death."

Jack pondered the attraction of a quick, clean death. He
was tired of feeling heat that radiated from everything,
eating the coarse, bitter grain that had been stored for the
horses, hearing the screams of dying children, and seeing
the wavering mirages of cool Canadian forests hovering in
the heat over the baked plain. Worst of all was the smell. It
hung over the entrenchment like a physical presence, a
hellish combination of sickness, decay, excrement and
death. In contrast, death seemed simple and attractive.
Finally, Jack understood Alice's reaction to Australian's
death. His horse *had* been lucky.

"I don't want to die." Jack croaked.

"Why not?"

"I'm in love."

"With the general's daughter?"

"Yes, with Alice Wheeler. She's the only person I've
met here who believes there is more to life than doing
things the right way and keeping up appearances in front
of the natives."

"She's an exceptional woman, right enough. But whatever she thinks, she is still the general's daughter and you
are a lowly 'alf-caste with no prospects nor suitable connec-
tions."

"But things will change." Jack's voice rose as he warmed
to his topic. "Look at our situation here. Everyone is in this

together, helping each other regardless of social position. Aunt Katherine was one of the worst for maintaining the social niceties and look at her now, helping anyone regardless of their place in society and doing things she would never have dreamed of doing before. How can she go back to the old ways?"

"You'd be surprised. As soon as the relief column arrives and contact is made with the outside world, all this camaraderie will collapse. The old 'abits will surface and friends who 'ave saved each other's lives will suddenly notice that they are not the same any more."

"I don't believe you." Jack felt his anger at Tommy's negativity rise again. "You're wrong. Things *will* change."

Tommy shrugged. "I've seen it 'appen before. In battle I am Subaltern Tommy Davies, a comrade and fellow soldier. In the mess after the victory I am a fishmonger's son who 'as risen above his position."

"But—" Jack could think of no good argument to refute what his friend was saying. "I think it will be different this time," he finished weakly, his anger vanishing once more.

"Oh, it might be different. Do you remember the Great Exhibition in London seven years ago?"

"Yes." Jack said. "It was in all the newspapers."

"Well, I went to it. It was full of wonders you cannot even imagine. One day, and not too far away, the world will be much smaller. It will be tied togevver by steam trains, steam ships, per'aps even 'orseless carriages that don't need to run on rails. Why, there is even talk of flying machines! And that's not all. The telegraph will go everywhere. It will be possible to send a message anywhere in the world in seconds. 'Ouses and streets will be lit with gas and, maybe even electric, lamps.

"We live in an extraordinary age of change. Things'll be very different, in our lifetimes. But what you can't change is people. There'll always be rich and poor, princes and paupers, generals' daughters and 'alf-caste soldiers' sons from the colonies."

Tommy sagged back in exhaustion. Jack began chuckling. Tommy stared at his friend. "What?"

Jack's laughter grew. "All your change and this wonderful world had better happen quickly. We'll all be dead in a week," he choked out.

Tommy smiled, caught up in Jack's laughter. "Perhaps Neill's building a railway to come and rescue us."

"Or, maybe he'll come in on a flying horseless carriage. We'd better clear the bodies away so he can land and save us."

The pair's hysterical laughter echoed over the oppressive hot silence of the entrenchment. Heads turned to listen, but no one joined in. It was just another fever victim descending into insanity.

Day 18: Tuesday, June 23

A word in your ear, O'Hara." Even in the dark, Jack recognized the tall figure of Gordon Wheeler. He was heading for one of Captain Moore's meetings in the ruins of the hospital barracks when the general's son stepped in front of him.

"I understand that you are spending a considerable amount of time in my sister's company?"

Jack felt anger rise. "In case you hadn't noticed, there are hundreds of us trapped here in a small area. It is difficult to avoid other people."

"Don't cheek me, boy," Gordon said coldly. "You know what I mean. Just because you have picked up some radical ideas in the Canadas doesn't mean you can come here and do what you want. You are to stay away from Alice; she is too good for you. You are nothing more than a no-account half-caste."

"Then that makes us equal," Jack spat back.

Jack was sure Gordon was going to hit him. He sensed the body before him tense and saw the fist raised. He stood his ground, waiting for the blow to fall, but Gordon turned on his heel and strode off.

Jack let out a long breath. His anger dissipated as quickly as it had arrived. He regretted what he had said; it would only make things worse. How was he going to be able to talk to Alice now? Apparently, the structure of European society hadn't broken down completely in the entrenchment. Perhaps if he apologized? Mentally kicking himself for his stupidity, Jack continued to the meeting.

"They will be attacking most violently today." Hari was almost invisible in the pre-dawn darkness. He had crept into the entrenchment half an hour earlier, terrifying a nervous sentry when he seemed to materialize beside the man with no warning. He had brought news that there would be no aid from Lucknow—Lawrence needed every man he had to defend the Residency there—but he had also heard talk of an assault on his way through the *sepoy* lines. Now he was huddled beneath a charred wall with Captain Moore, Gordon Wheeler and a number of other men, including Tommy and Jack.

"Finally," Moore said with savage glee. "At last we'll get a decent chance to have at them."

"Does this mean the relief column is near?" Gordon asked, voicing Jack's unspoken question.

"I fear it is not so," Hari replied. "They wish the utter destruction of you all today for the Battle of Plassey."

"Of course!" Moore exclaimed. "It's been a hundred years since old Clive sorted things out and got the Company on its feet. How Nana Sahib would love to win a victory today. But I say, let him come. We have teeth enough left to give him a nasty surprise."

"What's Plassey?" Jack whispered to Tommy.

"It was the Indian equivalent of Wolfe's victory on the Plains of Abraham—General Robert Clive's great victory over the Nawab of Bengal. Eight 'undred soldiers and two thousand two 'undred native troops defeated an army of fifty thousand and secured the East India Company's rule over India. Didn't they teach you anyffing of use in the Canadian wilderness?"

Jack ignored the dig. "Three thousand defeated fifty thousand?"

"The discipline and bravery of the British soldier can overcome extraordinary odds." Even in the darkness, Jack could feel Gordon Wheeler's stare.

"That's all true," Captain Moore broke in, "but even British bravery needs assistance sometimes. It helped that Clive had bribed most of the Nawab's army not to fight. That's something they don't teach here either."

The discussion was interrupted by a breathless sentry stumbling over the rubble. "Something's going on out there, sir," he addressed Moore. "Can't see much, but there's activity over by the native infantry lines."

"So, they think they can sneak up on us in the dark," Moore said as he stood up. "Let's go and see what's what. Wheeler, will you take Hari to report to the general and tell him I am going to investigate."

Jack thought he saw Gordon open his mouth to object, but all he did was salute and lead Hari into the deeper darkness.

The small party grabbed their muskets and headed over to the trenches where men were peering uneasily into the blackness.

"Looks like several hundred gathering for an attack, sir," one of them reported.

"Then let's give them a surprise before they do. You five men follow me." Moore indicated Tommy, Jack and three others. "When I begin giving words of command, spread out and make as much noise as possible. Then we'll give them a volley and withdraw."

Six against several hundred didn't seem like good odds to Jack, but he didn't have a chance to think about it. Moore crawled over the parapet with the others behind him. Jack had no choice, he couldn't desert his friends.

As silently as possible, the small group worked its way over the plain. Eventually, they could hear the noise of a sizable body of men in front of them.

We're dead, Jack thought, just before Moore's voice rang out with a string of clipped commands.

"First section halt.

"Second section, right about and turn to the left.

"Steady men. Fire on my command."

Jack shuffled to one side, banging his equipment against his musket and trying to sound like a lot more than one frightened boy.

The ruse worked. Thinking that they were surprised by a large force, the mutineers fled in disorder.

"Fire!" Moore commanded.

A ragged volley of six shots rang out.

"Time we got back now," Moore said in a quieter voice. "That should hold them till daybreak."

By dawn, the excitement of the nighttime success had worn off. Nothing had changed. It was going to be another hot, thirsty, hungry, uncomfortable day in the trenches and some more of the defenders were going to die.

"Can we stop an all-out attack?" Jack asked.

"Maybe," Tommy answered listlessly.

The pair was lying against the mud wall, primed muskets on either side. After Moore's excursion, they had barely had time for a drink of water and a bowl of rough gruel made from horse feed before they had to take their positions for the coming attack.

Jack looked over at his friend. Like everyone else, Tommy was skeletal, his eyes sunken and dark and his cheekbones pushing out against his burned and blistered skin. Angry red areas stood out on his face where blisters had burst, and his lips were cracked and raw.

Jack's irrational mood swings had become worse. One minute he would be cheerfully speculating on the imminent arrival of the relief column or helping calculate the rate of enemy fire with Tommy's precious watch; the next, for no apparent reason, he would be slumped in sullen silence, depressed and convinced that only a horrible death awaited them all. The only things that could lift one of Jack's black moods were thoughts of Alice, and now he had his meeting with Gordon Wheeler to complicate that.

With a conscious effort, Jack spoke to his friend. "What time is it?"

"Who cares?" Tommy replied.

"I care!" Jack said angrily. "Your dad gutted a lot of fish for that watch. The least you can do is use it when someone asks you the time."

Tommy opened his eyes and looked at Jack. Laboriously, he reached into his tattered tunic, produced the watch and opened it.

"'Alf past nine."

"Normally, I'd be coming back from my morning ride on Australian. I'd have a wash and then Aunt Katherine would make a cup of tea. She used to say that tea was the greatest drink ever invented—it warmed you in the cold and refreshed you in the heat."

"I think she's bringing us a cup now." Tommy said, looking across the entrenchment with sudden interest.

Jack caught sight of his aunt approaching from the tiled-roof barracks in a crouching run. The only dress she had left hung, ragged and bloodstained from her work in the hospital, and she was panting loudly with the exertion. She flopped into the trench beside her nephew.

"What are you doing here?" Jack asked.

"Word going round," Aunt Katherine said as she drew breath, "is that there is to be a big attack today. Some of the other women and I decided that we could be more use out here loading muskets for the men than cowering inside waiting for the worst. So here I am. Now, when they attack, you just pass the muskets back once you have fired them and I will load as fast as I can. I daresay, I'm not as efficient as you soldiers, but I think I can keep up."

Jack was stunned. Was this the same woman who had fussed endlessly about his behaviour? He was distracted by a short laugh from Tommy.

"I'm sure you can, ma'am. You're as keen as mustard. If everyone were like you, we could 'old out forever."

Where Soldiers Lie

Tommy replaced his watch and peered over the parapet. As rapidly as it had gone down, his mood had swung back up. "Now, Jack. Watch and listen and you might just learn someffing about soldiering. If I were leading the *sepoys* right now, I'd 'ave 'em form up behind the ruins of the church and sneak forward to the—"

All of a sudden, the cannonade increased dramatically. Musket balls thudded into the parapet, causing Tommy and Jack to duck back down hurriedly.

"'Ere we go," Tommy said. "It won't be long now. Remember, novices like yourself tend to fire 'igh in the 'eat of battle. Aim at the ground in front of a running man. Even if you fire low, the musket ball will ricochet up toward him. Also, when the cavalry charge, aim for the 'orse not the man. 'Orses are bigger targets and a cavalryman is no use without 'is 'orse."

Jack felt a thrill pass through him. Finally, after all the suffering, waiting and skirmishing, a real battle was about to begin. This would be his chance to hit back at the invisible forms that had been torturing him with cannon and musket shot for almost three weeks. Even though he might be dead in an hour or two, Jack felt more alive than ever. His senses were unnaturally sharp. He could hear a woman crying over by the ruined barracks, smell the smoke from the *sepoy*'s fires and feel the roughness of his clothes against his skin. In the remains of the verandah around the tiled barracks, he could see the two blond boys he had first noticed on the ride into the entrenchment crouching around some game in the dirt. He felt a wave of unreasoning delight pass through him that they should still be alive when so many children were dead. In that crystal moment, Jack was happy. As long as those boys survive, he thought, I shall be fine. As long as I am fine, Alice will be too. There will be a life after all this.

Jack's face was wreathed in a broad, idiotic grin when a nearby soldier yelled, "Here they come!"

Jack grabbed a loaded musket and peered out. Across the open ground, *sowars* were settling their horses while hundreds of *sepoys* formed up for a charge. In the wavering heat haze, they looked like skinny giants.

"Remember," Tommy said out of the side of his mouth, "aim low."

"Why aren't we firing on them?" Jack asked. The entrenchment cannons were silent despite the obvious target.

"They're too far off for our guns to do much damage. Once they charge, we will 'ave one or two chances to fire grape and canister into them. We 'ave to wait until they are close enough so that it will do the maximum damage."

Jack felt his mouth begin to dry out again. The waiting was the hardest.

All of a sudden, the *sowars* urged their mounts forward and began the long gallop toward the entrenchment. The *sepoys* loped along behind in a dense mass. It seemed to Jack as if the entire rebel army was charging straight at him—and they were coming with frightening speed.

"Why don't we fire?" Jack mumbled.

"Wait," Tommy replied.

To Jack's inexperienced military eye, it appeared as if the charging horsemen were about to leap the mud wall.

He could clearly see the horse's flared nostrils and the riders' open mouths as they screamed, *"Deen! Deen"* (For the Faith! For the Faith!) and waved their *tulwars* above their heads. Then, with a mighty roar, the cannons to Jack's right and left fired.

Thousands of grape-sized iron balls tore through the cavalry. Horses screamed and tumbled head over heels. Riders flew through the air or disappeared beneath the rolling bodies of their mounts. The solid wall of charging horses and men that Jack had thought unstoppable broke into small groups that seemed almost stunned. Here and there a rider continued his wild charge, only to be dropped by musket fire.

Jack aimed at a horseman riding diagonally across his front. The target was huge compared to the small deer he was used to shooting back in Canada West. Jack led the moving target, judging that his musket ball would strike where the horse's heart was. The musket crashed and a cloud of acrid smoke stung his nose and momentarily obscured his view. When it cleared, the horse lay still, crushing the rider's legs beneath its bulk.

Jack passed his musket back to his aunt and grabbed a fresh one. Now the *sepoys* were streaming through the chaos of the *sowars'* charge. Their presence seemed to settle the horsemen and, despite the heavy musket fire, they were reforming and joining the attack.

Jack leaned his musket on the wall and aimed at a large *sepoy* running straight at him. The man's red jacket was flapping wide as he ran, but Jack aimed at the centre of his body. He had a momentary image of the *sepoy*'s wide mustache streaming back as he ran, before he fired and smoke again obscured his view.

As he reached back for another musket, the cannons fired again. When the smoke cleared, Jack was amazed to see that the charge had disintegrated. Bloody piles of bodies, many still twitching, lay where the grapeshot had cut them down. Some *sepoys* were still running forward, their faces twisted in hate, but the Enfield muskets were picking them off with efficient regularity. The majority of the attackers were streaming back in a disorganized horde across the plain.

Jack fired a couple more shots at the retreating *sepoys* and, when there were no more living targets, slumped back into the trench. He felt elated at simply being alive. Intellectually, he knew he had killed men and the slaughter in front of the guns would normally have sickened him, but the adrenaline was still coursing through his body and he was overcome with wild excitement. The sharp smell of the gunpowder, the screams of the dying and the thump of the rebel cannonballs that were still landing in the entrenchment behind him all seemed perfectly fitted to his mood. He felt as if this was what he had been born for— to fight, and to win.

"We saw them off," he shouted at Tommy, now much more excited than his friend.

"We did that, but they'll be back."

"And we'll see them off again."

Tommy smiled, his teeth white against his smoke-blackened skin. "If they keep on making it easy for us."

"What do you mean?"

"They charged too early. The cavalry left the *sepoys* behind and the 'orses were already tired by the time we fired. That's why the charge broke up so easily."

"What should they have done?"

"The cavalry should have started slowly, kept the *sepoys* with them, and gradually built up speed. If they had timed it right, they would just 'ave been hitting the full gallop when we fired and we wouldn't 'ave slowed 'em near as much. Also, if the *sepoys* had kept up, they would 'ave been through the cavalry and at our trench before the cannon could 'ave been reloaded. Then it might 'ave been a different matter. It's really a disgrace; we trained them better than that."

"Well, I for one am glad they forgot their training," Aunt Katherine said as she primed muskets and laid them against the parapet. "Do you know that Captain Moore collected all the ladies stockings yesterday for the cannons?"

"Stockings?" Jack asked, vaguely shocked at his aunt talking about ladies's undergarments.

"Yes," Tommy explained. "The nine-pounder barrels 'ave been fired so much that they are distorted—oval now instead of round. The canisters of grape don't fit any more. It's an old dodge to wrap grape in material—stockings are perfect—so that it will fit in a worn barrel. As you saw, it works."

"What are those?" Aunt Katherine was peering past Jack and Tommy.

"Cunning devils," Tommy said as he looked over the parapet. "They're using cotton bales from the stores by the river for cover."

To Jack it looked as if huge snowballs were being rolled toward the trenches. Dark figures crowded behind them, occasionally darting out to fire their muskets. When they were about 350 yards away, the *sepoys* let out a wild shout and charged forward. Grape and musket fire cut them down and set several of the cotton bales on fire. The attack melted away as suddenly as it had formed, leaving smoking bales and more bloody figures scattered over the ground.

"That should 'old them for a while," Tommy said, grimly. "'Ot work, though."

"I must get back to the hospital," Aunt Katherine said. "There will be wounded now to attend to."

"I'll come with you," Jack said. "I'll get some water for us." And I'll see if Alice is all right, he added to himself.

Almost as if Jack had spoken aloud, Tommy added, "Best make sure that Alice Wheeler's all right while you're there."

Jack felt his face redden. Both Tommy and his aunt were smiling at him. "I ... I might," he stuttered.

"She's a nice girl," Aunt Katherine said, "and she cares for you."

"She what?" Jack couldn't believe what he was hearing.

"You're an intelligent boy, Jack," his aunt went on, "but you can be awfully dense about some things. Young Alice Wheeler is continually bothering me with questions about you. Are you safe? Are you going on any more raids? I can barely get any work done."

"She asks that?"

Aunt Katherine turned to Tommy. "Can you talk any sense into him?"

Tommy shook his head. "No room in there for sense, ma'am, it's all too full of lost cities. Besides, 'e thinks 'e ain't good enough for the general's daughter."

"A month ago I would have agreed," Aunt Katherine said with a wry smile, "But now? Things have changed so much. Everything has been turned upside down. I sometimes wonder if things will ever get back to the way they were before."

"I think they will go back to the way they were before," Jack said. "Gordon Wheeler has warned me off talking to Alice."

"Oh, he has, has he?" Aunt Katherine said. "Well, don't you pay too much attention to that. Gordon finds it difficult to fit in. Mind you, some of the cantonment women, and I suppose I am as much to blame as anyone, haven't made it easy for him. Don't you pay too much attention to him, Jack. These are unusual times and who knows what tomorrow might bring. Now, I really must be getting back."

Jack was too stunned to move. Alice cared for him and his aunt was supporting him instead of nagging him to do things properly!

"Well. There's a turn up for the book," Tommy said as Aunt Katherine made her way to the barracks. "With her on your side, nuffing can stop you now."

"Tommy, I think I'm falling in love with Alice."

"Oh, gawd!" Tommy exclaimed. "You look like a sick puppy and sound even worse. Go away before I 'ave to beat some sense into you."

In a half daze, Jack stood and stumbled over the open ground. In the barracks, he picked his way over the listless bodies sprawled in what little remained of the verandahs toward where the water cistern sat. It was hard to tell the living from the dead.

As he turned the corner by General Wheeler's room, Jack's stomach lurched in terror. Slumped against the wall, head drooping to the side and eyes closed, lay the blood-stained body of Alice.

"No!" he cried as he lunged forward.

To his immense relief, Alice's eyelids flickered and she raised her head.

Jack crouched beside her. "Where are you wounded?"

Alice's eyes were red with weeping and the dirt on her face was streaked with tears. "I'm not wounded."

"But the blood?"

Alice looked down at her torn and bloody dress as if noticing it for the first time. "Oh," she said, distantly. "That's not my blood."

"Whose?"

Tears welled in Alice's eyes. Each one rolling down her cheeks felt to Jack as if a dagger were being driven into him. She swallowed hard to regain control. "It's Gordon's. He was buckling on his sword when the attack began. A cannonball came through the wall. It—" She squeezed her eyes shut to force back another wave of tears and a shudder passed through her body. "It hit him in the head. I was sitting on the floor beside him. His body fell in my lap."

Jack was horrified. He had seen what a cannonball could do to a man's head.

Alice gave in to the tears and leaned into Jack's shoulder. Tentatively, he placed his arm around her in what he hoped was a comforting gesture. They sat there in the late morning heat, a sculpture of sorrow.

Jack's mind was in turmoil. He felt shock at Gordon Wheeler's death, anger at the mutineers who had killed him and sorrow for Alice's loss. But most of all he felt a guilty happiness that these circumstances had led to him sitting in the dirt holding Alice Wheeler.

Day 20: Thursday, June 25

I wish they would come closer." Tommy gazed longingly at the plump dogs scavenging among the scattered, decomposing bodies left after the attack of two days before. "If only we had someffing to entice them close enough for a clean shot. There's a good stew in one of them."

"They've got all they can eat out there," Jack replied bleakly. "They're better fed than we are with our horse rations. How much longer can we hold out?"

Tommy continued to lean on the parapet, gazing hungrily at the dogs. "Who knows. There's more than 350 of us stuffed down that well yonder, which leaves less than seven 'undred. 'Course only about two 'undred are fighting men and some of them are barely strong enough to raise their muskets. There's only an 'andful of gunners left, but that's no matter, I doubt any of the cannon could fire more than two or three shots at most. The burned-out barracks provide precious little shelter and the tiled barracks are so riddled with shot 'oles that it'll most likely collapse in a day or two. We've got food, if you can call it that, for a few days yet, but it is a big question whether anyone will remain alive long enough to eat it."

"So we're in good shape then," Jack said through cracked lips.

Tommy laughed shortly. "We are. Those mutineers are exactly where we want them. All we 'ave to do is—"

Jack looked up at his friend's silence. "What? Are they coming again?"

"Well, someone is."

Jack pulled himself up to peer over the parapet. It took him a minute to find what his friend had seen, but at last he made out a lone figure, approaching on foot across the plain. Almost at the same moment, he realized that the barrage had stopped. Jack lifted his musket and aimed at the figure. "I have a rupee says I can drop him with one shot."

"It's a woman," Tommy said. "She's waving. Go and tell Captain Moore that someone's coming in."

Leaving his musket, Jack staggered over to the barracks. He met Moore coming out of the main door. "There's a woman coming in from the *sepoy* lines, sir."

"That might explain why the barrage has stopped. Let's see what she wants."

By the time they returned to the trenches, Tommy was helping an old woman over the parapet.

"Welcome to our humble abode," Moore said. "Who are you and what brings you here?"

The woman looked around at the gaunt faces staring back at her. Despite her age and the grubby state of her clothes, she held herself proudly erect. "I am Rose

Greenaway," she said, in a commanding voice. "My sons, Thomas and Samuel are, I believe, within your entrenchment. My third son, Edward, and I were captured at our indigo factory on June the eighth. Since then, we have been the prisoners of Nana Sahib, pending the payment of a ransom to ensure our safe passage to Allahabad. I have a letter for General Wheeler."

Moore took the offered sheet and unfolded it. From his position slightly behind the captain, Jack could see what was written on it. The script was immaculate, but the message brief: "To the subjects of Her Most Gracious Majesty Queen Victoria. All those who . . . are willing to lay down their arms, shall receive a safe passage to Allahabad."

The word "safe" leaped off the page at Jack. A truce! They were being offered a way out. Maybe this was the end. Maybe, in just a few days, they would be sitting eating a real meal in Allahabad. The idea was intoxicating. He wanted to scream, "Yes! Yes! We accept." But the decision wasn't up to him.

Moore gazed at the note for a long minute, then he folded it and addressed their visitor. "Thank you for conveying this to us. A response will require some discussion. We can offer you little in the way of hospitality, but I am sure you would welcome the chance to become reacquainted with your two sons. Please follow me."

How could Moore remain so calm? Jack's heart was pounding in his chest as loud as an artillery barrage. Jack exchanged a glance with Tommy. His eyes were bright with excitement. Since no one told them not to, Tommy and Jack followed the captain across the compound.

A hurried meeting was convened in General Wheeler's room. Jack hovered in the background, beside a large patch of dried blood that he morbidly thought must have belonged to Gordon. There was no sign of Alice.

"It is monstrous," General Wheeler opened the discussion. "The note is not even signed and it is by no means clear. We must fight on and trust in the relief column."

"I concur," a tall officer with a filthy bandage around his head added. "It would be a disgrace to surrender. Better to die with a sword in our hand than give in to this rabble."

"And we must not forget that Nana Sahib has betrayed us once already," a second officer contributed. "How can we trust him now?"

"If we surrender," Lieutenant Boulton said, "we give strength to the enemy. Nana Sahib will trumpet his victory across North India. Who knows how many more will join the mutiny because of it. Our surrender will make Lawrence's job at Lucknow that much more difficult."

Murmurs of assent ran around the room. Jack was horrified—they were going to fight on. He turned to Captain Moore, who had been silent until now. He took an age to answer, looking, Jack thought, as if there were a great weight on his shoulders.

"I detest the idea of surrender," Moore began slowly. "I think I have demonstrated over the last weeks as much willingness to fight as any man." There were nods of agreement. "If it were only I and my brave companions, I would fight on and take as many of the mutineers to hell with me as I could, but it is not only myself that I speak for and I must counsel an honourable course.

"Our situation is hopeless. The rains could begin at any moment, rusting our muskets and washing away our defences in a single night. Another day of heavy bombardment and the barracks will collapse upon itself and the poor wretches within. We have no medicine, instruments or shelter with which to give the sick and wounded even the most basic succour. We have food left for only three more days and hardly enough shot to repel one more concerted attack. It is not a question of a soldier's honour. We must think of the women and children. This may be the only opportunity to save their lives."

"But the relief column could be here in three days," the tall officer blurted out.

Moore stared hard at him. "The relief column has not yet left Allahabad."

A shocked gasp met the news.

"But that's not possible," the tall officer said. "Neill has been at Allahabad since June 11. Surely he must be closer now."

"He is not. We received news in the night that Havelock's column from Calcutta is still a week away from Allahabad and Neill will not move until it arrives. We cannot hope for relief before the second or third week of July. By then we will all be long dead."

A stunned silence met Moore's brutal assessment of their hopeless situation. Jack's first reaction was horror, but then his spirits rose. The news would force a surrender after all.

Eventually, Wheeler spoke. "That's it then. We must negotiate the best possible capitulation. Please see to the negotiations, Captain Moore."

"Very good, sir. I suggest that an acceptable minimum is that we must have covered boats and boatmen, both of which must be inspected beforehand. There must be provisions enough for the journey, transportation for the sick and wounded to the boats at Sati Chowra Ghat and, if possible, we must be allowed to retain some arms and ammunition for our defence on the journey. In exchange we will abandon the entrenchment, all our heavy weapons and what money and valuables we have stored here."

General Wheeler nodded acquiescence. "Please compose a letter to that effect for Mrs. Greenaway to take back."

Moore saluted briskly and left.

Jack and Tommy wandered out of the barracks into the eerie silence and savoured the feeling of being able to stand in the open without being shot at.

"It's over. Just like that," Jack said. The speed with which things had changed almost overwhelmed him. "Can we trust Nana Sahib?"

"I don't know," Tommy answered, "but as Moore pointed out so eloquently, we 'ave little choice." He kicked the dry ground in a sudden burst of anger. "Damn Neill to 'ell. 'E could 'ave been 'ere by now. Instead 'e dawdles in Allahabad, 'anging mutineers and waiting for 'Avelock."

"Perhaps he needs the reinforcements."

"'E needs courage not reinforcements!" Tommy scoffed. "Two 'undred disciplined troops with a few guns could walk 'ere from Allahabad in a week. Can you see Moore in Neill's place? Would 'e not move 'eaven and earth to relieve us or die trying?"

Jack had to admit that he would rather Moore were in

Allahabad than Neill.

As word of Rose Greenaway's visit spread and the silence of the cannons lengthened, more and more people emerged to savour the unusual feeling of standing up in the open in safety. It was not the cheering celebration it should have been—the ragged, starved look of the survivors suggesting more that the graves of a cemetery had opened and allowed the occupants to stagger out. Ladies who, a few short weeks ago, would have been mortified to be seen in anything but the most elaborate creation of petticoats, lace and silk, scrabbled to pull a few filthy rags together to cover their nakedness. Men accustomed to the rugged pursuits of hunting tiger and crocodile tottered around on skeletal limbs over which skin, burned almost black by the sun, stretched like fragile parchment. All gazed at each other through sunken eyes and wondered if their cheeks were as hollow, their teeth as yellow, or their hair as filthy and bloodied as those they saw around them.

Worst were the emaciated children. Some ran about with unnatural nervous energy in a pitiful parody of play. Others dragged listlessly behind parents or, if they had been orphaned, any adult who had shown them kindness. A few seemed to be behaving normally. Jack watched the two blond boys playing tag, laughing and shouting with glee. Maybe they were the lucky ones.

Almost three weeks of siege had reduced the survivors of the entrenchment to a pitiable state, one that seemed all the worse now that they were apparently safe. People gravitated almost unconsciously toward the well where they could, at last, drink their fill in safety. Some were even attempting to wash the grime of the siege off. Jack spotted his aunt walking with Alice.

"I see my aunt," Jack said. "I think I'll go and talk with her."

"I think she is not the only person you see," Tommy said. "Make the most of it. I must go and check the sentries. Just because we are negotiating with the rebels, we shouldn't let our guard down."

Tommy moved away and Jack walked over to the two women. "You've heard the news?" he asked.

"We have," Aunt Katherine replied. "I think it is splendid that sense has prevailed at last. Many of the sick and wounded would not have survived much longer. Is it true that provisioned boats are to be provided tomorrow?"

"It is being negotiated. I don't know if everything will be organized by tomorrow." Although he was talking to his aunt, Jack couldn't keep his eyes off Alice. She looked happier than when he had last seen her, but there was a sadness to her downcast eyes that made Jack want to take her in his arms.

"Well," Aunt Katherine said, seeing that she was not the centre of Jack's attention. "I think I will enjoy a stroll around the perimeter before I return to the hospital."

As his aunt moved away, Alice raised her eyes and looked at Jack. "Thank you for comforting me the other day." Even sunken above her hollow cheeks, Alice's eyes were beautiful.

"I'm happy to do anything to help." Jack meant it. He would have walked across hot coals for her, and the thought that he and she might soon be moving in mutually exclusive social circles hurt. He struggled to think of something to say.

Before he came up with anything, Alice went on. "Gordon and I were very close when I was little. He was the big brother who protected me, picked me up when I fell and dried my tears. We became less close as he grew older. The army became his life. It was a way he could define himself and not have to think too much about how we didn't fit in. It's funny, but when he was younger, he didn't want to join the army, but father insisted."

"What did he want to do?"

"He loved the country. Where so many Europeans simply see the dirt and confusion, he saw a rich history and a vibrant culture. He used to tell me that India would be a wonderful place to study the past because the Indians don't feel our need to destroy what is old in order to build something new. They just change its use. That is why there are so many old forts, palaces—even entire abandoned cities—still standing. We used to play a game where we would guess what of our presence in India would still be here one hundred years after we have gone."

Jack was fascinated by this portrait of Gordon, so different from the person he had met. "Do you think the mutiny will drive us out?" he asked.

"Oh, no. Havelock and the army will put down the mutiny, whatever happens here. India is too important to the Empire. We will stay."

"For how long?"

"A hundred years. Maybe two. But, remember, India has been here for thousands of years. There's a lot here today that Alexander the Great would still recognize. We're just one more invader."

"But aren't we bringing progress—science and new inventions that will revolutionize the world?"

"I don't have your faith in progress. For every safer way to get from one place to another, there will be a bigger, more accurate gun that will be able to kill more people. Sometimes I wonder if we weren't better off in caves when we could only hit each other on the head with rocks."

Jack was shocked at the idea. "But progress is inevitable. How else will we improve the world?"

"Has gunpowder improved the world?"

"To some degree, yes. It has made building roads and railways much easier."

"But it has also made killing much easier. Perhaps we need to improve people before we talk about improving the world."

Alice saw the look of confused anger cross Jack's face. "But I don't want to argue with you. Tell me about the Canadas where you grew up. I hear it is a huge empty land."

For what seemed to be an age, Jack chatted happily about his years growing up, snowshoeing in the winter, canoeing in the summer, hunting in the woods to his heart's content. But he was talking about a foreign land.

"It's not my home, though," he ended his description rather lamely.

"Where is?"

"Here, I suppose. Odd, I've only been here a year and, half the time, I still have no idea what's going on."

Alice laughed lightly. "You're not alone. You begin by hating India—the noise, the dirt, the crowds—but before you know it, it's wormed its way under your skin and you are hooked. All the Europeans here talk about England as home, but very few ever go back. They ache with nostalgia for London or Bournemouth, but they die in Simla or Calcutta. Welcome to India."

"But society here is so rigid."

"Then leave it. You will never be a proper sahib anyway. Your skin, like mine, is too dark. If you want to stay in India, you will have to find your own way—perhaps go off searching for your lost cities."

"Will you stay?"

"Of course. Where else could I go?"

"But not as a memsahib?"

"No. My dream is to learn Sanskrit so that I can study the Vedas. I could happily live my life in a dusty library."

"The Vedas would be your lost city."

"Yes." Alice smiled. "And if I find your city in there, I shall be sure to tell you."

"I hope we can still meet after this is all over," Jack blurted out.

Alice regarded him with a penetrating stare. "I would like that," she said eventually. "But now I must go and help Mother."

Jack stood beside the well, watching Alice walk toward the barracks. He was aching, hungry, tired and by no means certain what the future might hold, but this was the happiest moment of his life.

Day 21: Friday, June 26

Jack stood in the fading evening light looking over the open ground at the ragged figures clustered around the sepulchral well. The padre was conducting a farewell service for those who had been so unceremoniously buried. One by one, people stepped forward and gently dropped a scrawled memorial or a keepsake to lie with their loved ones in the monstrous hole. Everyone held a handkerchief or scrap of cloth to their nose as they approached.

Jack thought of the well's contents—soldiers, civilians, women and children—intertwined democratically in death. The well was a history of the siege—at the bottom lay Charles Hillersdon, Lydia and their baby, killed so long ago when death was still shocking; near the top lay the headless body of Gordon Wheeler. Between them were hundreds of others, a pillar of agonizing loss that would forever memorialize the siege.

The day had been spent preparing for the departure tomorrow morning. Negotiations for the surrender had been finalized and a delegation of officers had been taken to inspect the boats drawn up by Sati Chowra Ghat. They had pronounced them adequate, although there was concern over the long way they would have to be poled across the river to reach the deep water channel close to the opposite bank. No one had much baggage, but treasured trinkets had been recovered from hiding places and sewn into clothing. Soldiers were allowed to keep their weapons and sixty rounds of ammunition, but all the cannons had been hauled away from the entrenchment. This made several of the officers nervous about a possible attack, but three of Nana's officials had agreed to stay the night in the entrenchment as hostages. If treachery was planned, then it was an extremely elaborate ruse.

Alice, Aunt Katherine and the other women had been busy preparing the wounded for the one-mile journey to the river. About a dozen were so badly wounded that they could not be moved and would have to be left to an unknown fate.

The unaccustomed silence of the past two days weighed on Jack. It seemed almost unnatural after the chaotic noise of the siege. It had also encouraged the vultures to return and they waddled about the open ground feasting on what the dogs had left. Jack gazed at the huge red sun lowering toward the horizon. Was it all over? Were they safe?

As if in answer, a familiar soft voice said, "Greetings, sahib."

Jack turned to see Hari's skinny figure standing beside him. Hari was dressed in a traditional loose cotton shirt and *dhoti* and carried a bundle of clothes.

"Hello, Hari," Jack said with a smile. "So, it is all over at last. You will have some stories to tell."

Hari's head bobbed. "Not so much, but I hear stories in the bazaar."

"What stories?"

"The soldiers are to be killed, sahib."

A chill ran down Jack's spine. "We are to be betrayed?"

Again the nod. "It is talk, but many say so. I bring you the clothes of a servant. Your skin is dark. Come with me tonight and I will take you where it is safe."

Jack stared at Hari in confusion. What was he offering— escape from a trap or entrance into more danger? If treachery was planned, why had it not happened already? They had been defenceless since the cannon had been removed.

As if in answer, a musket shot cracked out in the gathering gloom. It was followed by a fusillade of shots. Musket balls thudded into the barrack walls and the dry ground. Pandemonium erupted around Jack. Soldiers, cursing and grabbing muskets, rushed to the trench. Women and children, used again to safety, screamed in panic and fled to whatever shelter they could find.

Suddenly Tommy was at Jack's side. "Looks like it's not over yet," he said, grabbing his friend's sleeve. "Come on. Let's give as good an account of ourselves as we can."

Followed by Hari, Tommy and Jack piled into the trench and peered over the open ground. Jackals slunk away into the darkness and fat vultures struggled to rise into the air, but there was no screaming horde of attackers, although musket balls and occasional round shot still thudded into the ruined entrenchment.

"What does it mean?" Jack asked.

Hari shrugged. "It is an attack."

Tommy glanced at Hari. "Well, we will make the devils pay dearly for it."

However, no attack was forthcoming and, gradually, the firing died away. Word was passed along that it had been a mistake. A *sepoy*'s musket had fired by accident and triggered the outbreak. But, coming on top of what Hari had said, Jack was nervous.

"Hari says we are to be betrayed," he told Tommy. "He says the soldiers are to be killed."

"Nonsense!" Tommy said, looking hard at Hari who was nodding vigorously. "There is no reason to kill us now that we 'ave surrendered. And why did the firing stop just now? If they intended to kill us, they could walk in and get it over with in 'alf an hour. Besides, we 'ave no choice."

"I suppose," Jack said, not entirely convinced. "Have you told Captain Moore?" he added turning to Hari.

"I have, sahib. He is of the opinion of your friend. The choices are little for so many. That is why I came to you." Hari held out the bundle of clothes.

Jack was sorely tempted, not just because of what Hari had told them, but he was being offered something he had often dreamed of—an opportunity to escape the world of his aunt and become absorbed into the world of India. With Hari to guide him, he wouldn't have to worry about not understanding the caste system. His hand, almost of its own volition, reached slowly toward the bundle. Then Jack pulled it back. Only one thing was stopping him: Alice Wheeler. Jack would give up everything to stay with her and, if there was treachery planned, she would need protection. Jack's fantasy of rescuing Alice from danger was stronger than his dream of living like a native. Slowly he shook his head.

Hari shrugged almost apologetically and retreated into the gathering dark. Jack wondered if he would ever see him again.

"Is it going to be all right?" Jack asked.

"I don't know." Tommy's tone was so different from the confidence he had displayed recently that Jack looked at him. "There are so many stories going around. One of the officers inspecting the boats says 'e 'eard the word 'massacre' used. Some people believe it. One family even gave their infant girl to their nanny to take into the native city for safety."

"What do you think?"

"I think someffing's planned, but not the 'olesale massacre some fear. I think they may try and separate the soldiers tomorrow, but the women, children and civilians will be allowed to go downriver."

Jack pondered what his friend was suggesting and what it meant for them.

"That's why I want you to promise someffing." Tommy's voice was quiet and unusually serious. "If anything 'appens to me, take me old kettle and see that it gets back to me dad?"

"Nothing's going to happen."

"In that case, you won't 'ave to do anyffing and we can laugh about this in Allahabad."

"I will." Jack said seriously.

"Good," Tommy said, perking up. "I'm sure you are right. I am just croaking on. It's a soldier's 'abit.

"So the siege of Cawnpore is over. Who'd have thought we could have held out for twenty-one days in these conditions. But we gave a good account of ourselves, did we not?"

"We did," Jack replied, smiling at his friend's suddenly returned enthusiasm.

"And some good has come out if it."

"What?"

"You 'ave found turtle dove, of course."

"Love? I suppose I have," Jack said, thoughtfully.

"I envy you the object of your affection," Tommy said, patting his friend on the shoulder, "but I fear the struggle that faces you once things are back to normal will make the siege look like a picnic."

"Maybe not. She wants to study ancient Indian writings and I want to discover lost cities. We could do that together, away from all the nonsense of sahibs and memsahibs." It was an idea that had been forming in Jack's mind since his conversation with Alice the day before. Why wouldn't it be possible?

"You're a dreamer, Jack O'Hara. Do you imagine for a moment that you will be allowed to just go off with Alice Wheeler and do whatever you want? If you do, you 'aven't learned much about this country. You are talking about going native and that is the last thing the sahibs and memsahibs will let you do. It looks bad—lets the side down. And if you think they'll let you take the general's daughter, 'owever dark her skin, to live in a mud village somewhere, you are very much mistaken. Society 'ere is as rigid as the clockwork in me kettle and they won't let you upset it."

"Why do you have to be so negative?" Jack was furious. If there was one person he wanted to believe in his dream, it was Tommy. "Nothing different would ever get done if it were up to you. You just want to live in the army where everything is decided for you and you don't have to think. You've no more imagination than the fish your father guts."

The look of hurt on Tommy's face made Jack instantly regret what he had said.

"I must go and check the sentries," Tommy said, coldly.

Jack watched his friend retreat. "I'm sorry," he said, but he couldn't tell if Tommy had heard him.

Jack punched the crumbling mud wall beside him. Why was life so complicated? The siege was barely over and already the outside world was pushing in on him. Jack had imagined the end of the siege many times—the absence of cannonballs and musket shot, the ability to walk around in the open, no more noise, stench and sudden death. He had prayed for those things and believed that, when that time came, everything would be fine. But it wasn't going to be. Tommy was right—his relationship with Alice, however radical and outspoken she was, was doomed. In some ways, crouching behind a mud wall, shooting at men who were trying to kill you was easier. Jack could see the attraction of the army life.

Disconsolately, he curled himself into a ball at the bottom of the trench and tried to sleep. Tomorrow it would all be over.

PART IV

The Vultures Feast

Saturday, June 27

An elephant had been supplied for General Wheeler and it led the way now, cutting a swaying path through the crowd of onlookers curious to watch the *feringhees* depart. Wheeler's family, including Alice, sat on the howdah on the beast's back, but the general himself rode a skinny pony to one side. Behind him, his senior officers, dressed in as much of their formal uniforms as had survived the siege, followed in ragged formation. Behind them, stretching almost half the distance back to the entrenchment, straggled everyone else, about seven hundred as close as anyone could tell, most walking but with the wounded in carts and carriages. Jack walked with his aunt immediately behind the officers.

The crowd mostly watched the wretched parade in silence. Occasionally, someone recognized a former master and called out a greeting or a curse. Jack saw a *sepoy* make a grab for an officer's musket.

"You may not have the musket," the officer shouted, levelling his weapon, "but you may have the contents." The *sepoy* backed off.

Moore was everywhere, cajoling, organizing and encouraging. "We must stick together on the road but when we get to the river, as soon as each boat is filled, pole it out into the deep water. Don't wait for others."

To a crowd of threatening *sepoys*, he shouted: "Your triumph will be short lived. In time every man will pay dearly for his misdeeds." The *sepoys* responded with profanities in Hindi and broken English.

"This will be our *Via Dolorosa*," Aunt Katherine said sadly.

"What is the *Via Dolorosa*?" Jack asked.

"Good God! Your education is sadly lacking. The *Via Dolorosa*—the way of sadness—was the route through Jerusalem that Christ took with his cross."

"But he died at the end."

"Yes," Aunt Katherine said. Before Jack could ask what she meant, she continued. "At the river, find that young officer friend of yours and get into the general's boat. Captain Moore and the other officers will be there. They will have the best chance."

"Best chance?"

"Just do as I say!" Aunt Katherine's imperious tone was back.

"All right," Jack agreed. "We will make for the general's boat."

"Do not wait for me," his aunt ordered. "I am too old to go looking for a specific boat. I will get in the one closest to shore."

"But—" Jack began to protest.

"Alice Wheeler will be in the general's boat."

Jack fell silent. He certainly wanted to be in the same boat as Alice.

The long procession wound down the ravine through the banks of the Ganges toward the river. Crowds lined the cliff tops, peering between the palm trees leaning out over the edge. Beneath the dome of the Hardeo Temple, several of Nana Sahib's officers sat in regal splendour as if overseeing the activities.

"It's such a beautiful spot," Aunt Katherine said, wistfully. "James used to bring me here for morning rides and picnics in the cool weather."

The place didn't look beautiful to Jack. The sandbars, dotted with dark pats of cow dung, stretched a long way out into the river. He was relieved to see about twenty-four boats drawn up in a rough line on several of the intricate channels, but they were discouragingly far off, and many were almost high and dry in little more than two feet of water. They would have to be manhandled a long way over to deep water. Jack hoped the survivors had enough strength. A few *sowars* rode about in the shallows, ordering the boatman to make last-minute preparations.

The boats were large—thirty feet long by about ten wide, Jack estimated. Each had a rough decking of bamboo poles and a thatched roof to protect the occupants from the sun. Two or three boatmen stood on each, clutching long, ungainly bamboo oars. The boats looked frighteningly fragile.

The Wheelers dismounted from their elephant and set out across the sandbars. The following throng funnelled down the ravine and spread out over the river toward the boats.

Aunt Katherine sat down heavily on a rock at the foot of the temple wall. "Go on," she wheezed. "You need to get there before the boat fills up and pushes off. Save me a spot, I'll be along just behind you."

Jack hesitated, torn between concern for his aunt and worry about missing the boat.

"Go on!" his aunt ordered firmly. "I'll just catch my breath and follow on. I've never been good in this damned heat."

"All right. I'll stand on the edge of the boat and wave so you can see which one I am on. Come as quick as you can."

Katherine nodded. "I'll be fine," she said with a smile.

As Jack turned away, she called to him. "You're a good boy, Jack. I'm sorry India has turned out like this for you, but I am very proud of you. Remember that."

Jack hesitated, but she waved him away.

The going was hard as the weakened survivors trudged through sand or waist-deep water. Several sat down in exhaustion while others encouraged them to keep going.

About halfway to the boats, Jack noticed a *sowar* sitting on his horse nearby watching him. The man was dressed in the usual mixture of uniform and civilian clothes and carried a *tulwar* by his side. He wore a wide turban that slouched forward and obscured much of his face, yet there was something familiar about the man. As Jack stared, the man nodded at him, an almost apologetic twist of the head that could mean yes or no equally, then he turned his horse and splashed away through the shallows.

"Hari!" Jack shouted, but the crowd closed around him, jostling him forward.

Jack had no time to wonder why Hari was playing the part of a cavalryman as he worked his way to the Wheelers' boat. It was sitting in slightly deeper water than the others, but the keel was still resting on sand. Jack reached up to pull himself over the side.

"Come on, Jackie boy," hands grabbed Jack's wrists and hauled him up.

Jack found himself standing on the rough bamboo decking facing Tommy. He hadn't seen him since their argument the previous evening.

"Tommy, about last night. I—"

"There's no time for that now," Tommy cut him off, all business. "We've got to get this boat over to the deeper water."

Captain Moore and several other officers were trying to organize the occupants, ushering the women and children into the centre of the boat, below the decking. General Wheeler stood by the crude mast, gazing back at the shore. There was no sign of Alice.

"Come along," Moore urged. "We need to get loaded then push this contraption into deeper water."

Jack moved up to the stern, which was raised slightly, giving him a better view to look out for Aunt Katherine. He stood beside one of the boatmen and looked back over the sandbars. Hundreds of the bedraggled survivors of the entrenchment were struggling toward the boats. Some helped the injured or exhausted, others stumbled forward in a daze. Beside Jack, the other boats were filling rapidly.

Jack searched for Aunt Katherine. Eventually, he saw her. She was standing but still close to the mouth of the ravine. Jack groaned, he had hoped she would be well on her way by now. He should go and help her.

"Don't leave until I get back," he said in Hindi to the boatman.

The man started at the sound of Jack's voice. He gave Jack one fearful glance and fixed his gaze back on the Hardeo Temple. Jack followed his stare. He was aware of a commotion at the foot of the ravine, several *sowars* were riding about, waving the crowd of onlookers back, but his attention was held by a tall figure dressed in startlingly white clothes and standing on the temple steps. He had to be one of Nana Sahib's officers. Almost leisurely, the man waved a coloured scarf over his head. It was a signal. A bugle call rang out and three gunshots echoed from downstream. Instantly, the boatman flung his bamboo oar over the side and leapt into the water. He was followed by others all along the line of boats.

Jack stood stunned, watching the half-naked men stumble away through the shallows. Time slowed and a heavy silence descended like a blanket. People stood immobile, looking around in puzzlement. As if in a dream, a line of *sepoys* emerged from the palm trees on top of the bank and raised their muskets. Beside the temple, two small cannons were manhandled into position. Jack felt a hideous knot form in the pit of his stomach as realization overwhelmed him—Hari had been right, they had been betrayed.

"Run!" Jack yelled at Aunt Katherine, although she had no chance of hearing him.

Where Soldiers Lie

A crowd of women milled about the edge of the river in confusion. Several *sowars* nearby drew their swords. Jack searched for Hari among them, but they all looked the same. He had a horrible feeling of helplessness as the *tulwars* glinted in the sun. The swords fell and people screamed. Jack saw his aunt begin a staggering run toward the boats. "Hurry!" he urged under his breath, but it was useless. A *sowar* rode at Aunt Katherine from the side. She saw him and raised her arms in a futile attempt at defence. The razor-sharp weapon slashed down, taking both her pleading hands off at the wrists. Aunt Katherine stood for a moment, the stumps of her arms held up, before the return slash caught her at the base of the neck and her body collapsed into the bloody water like a rag doll.

Jack screamed, "No!"

A musket shot exploded beside him and one of the running boatmen catapulted forward. Then the *sepoys* along the bank fired. Panicked women and children struggled forward, shrieking as musket balls plowed into their backs. A cannonball smashed into the boat beside Jack, punching a gaping hole in the hull, tearing both legs off a soldier in the midst of climbing aboard. Without a sound, the man's body slid back into the water and sank.

"Aunt Katherine!" Jack felt an overwhelming sense of guilt at having abandoned his aunt to her ghastly fate. He pushed his way back to where the gunwales of the boat were lowest and began climbing over the side.

"What're you doing?" Tommy said, grabbing Jack's arm.

"Aunt Katherine."

"You can't 'elp her now. We 'ave to get the boat away, it's our only chance."

As Jack hesitated, Captain Moore was shouting orders. "Throw everything over the side. We must lighten her to get into deeper water."

A soldier beside Jack sighed and collapsed to the deck, a bright red hole in his temple.

"Get him over the side," Moore ordered.

Without questioning, Tommy and Jack manhandled the body out of the boat.

Moore and Lieutenant Boulton, the man who had vaulted into the entrenchment so long ago, leapt into the waist-deep water and put their backs to the hull. The vessel rocked, but a second volley from the shore caught both officers across their chests and they sank in a spreading patch of red.

Even with all that was going on around him, Jack was shocked. Moore had been such a force in the siege that he had seemed immortal. Now he was gone. Jack stared at the swirling, red water.

"Come on," Tommy said. "We've got to get the boat off."

Jack followed his friend over the side. He was vaguely aware of other figures splashing into the water around him.

"'Eave," Tommy exhorted, putting his shoulder to the rough wooden planking.

Jack felt slivers scratch his skin as he pushed. Musket balls splashed in the water all around and thudded into the wood by his head. The boat moved a couple of feet before grounding again.

"Once more!" Tommy shouted.

The boat shuddered and, suddenly, drifted free. Hands reached down and hauled the men in the water back on board. But the weight was too much and the craft again lurched to a stop.

By now, *sepoys* were running down the bank and *sowars* were riding through the shallows slashing wildly about them. Most of the boats were scattered, hopelessly stranded, some destroyed by cannon fire, others blazing fiercely. Terrified groups huddled behind them sheltering from the musket fire. Over the scene, clouds of black, acrid smoke drifted from the fires, catching the back of Jack's throat. The smoke obscured some of the horror but framed other tragic episodes.

Jack saw the regimental paymaster stagger across his view, one arm cut off at the shoulder. A headless body stood alone, balanced for what seemed like an age, before pitching forward.

Amidst it all, Jack saw the two blonde boys, holding hands and walking untouched through it all as if invisible.

"I must stop this." Jack looked up to see General Wheeler deliberately climbing over the side. He was followed by Lady Wheeler.

"Sir! Come back," an officer called out.

Wheeler turned and looked up at the boat. "I must talk to Nana Sahib," he said calmly. "There has been some mistake."

Everyone on the boat stood watching in awe as Lady Wheeler took her husband's arm and, together, the old couple walked away into the smoke, past the bloody bodies of the people who had trusted the general to protect them.

"Father!" The scream ripped through Jack like a knife. Alice Wheeler tore frantically up from below decks and, without hesitating, plunged over the side. Equally impulsively, Jack leaped after her.

He caught up with Alice just as she drew level with her parents.

"Father! Stop!"

The old general ignored his daughter and continued his plodding course. Over her shoulder, Lady Wheeler said, "He is determined. We shall meet our end this way. You and your young friend should go back to the boat."

"Not without you," Alice cried.

Jack had no idea what to do. He couldn't imagine physically forcing Alice back to the boat and nothing he could think of saying would persuade her to leave her parents.

Several nearby *sepoys* stopped their tasks of robbing the dead and dispatching the wounded and watched the tiny group's progress. None made a move against them, either out of a lingering respect for the general or because they could not believe their eyes.

They were about halfway back to the ravine, wading through a waist-deep channel, when a *sowar* burst toward them, bloodied sword raised high.

This is the end, Jack thought as the fearsome rider approached.

He never heard the musket shot that catapulted the attacker backward off his mount. The riderless horse continued on its way, crashing into the group and hurling Jack and Alice aside.

As if awakened by the shot, the nearby *sepoys* grabbed their muskets and poured a ragged volley into General Wheeler and his wife. Still holding hands, the pair sagged forward and sank.

Alice groaned and began pushing herself forward through the water.

"I don't think so, miss." Jack turned to see Tommy standing behind him. "We've got to get you away from 'ere.

"Do you know 'ow to use one of these?" Tommy handed Jack a curved cavalry sabre.

"No, but I'll learn."

"Good." Tommy held a musket with a long bayonet on the end. "We'll make for that wrecked boat first."

Dragging the unresisting Alice with his free hand, Jack followed Tommy toward the nearest burning hulk. Fortunately for the three, the *sepoys* seemed occupied with stripping the General and Lady Wheeler's bodies in a frantic search for hidden valuables.

Over behind the boat, they had a chance to assess the situation. The padre, half a dozen girls from a local school and several other terrified civilians were already there, crouching in fear. The boat Jack and Tommy had left appeared to be afloat, but *sowars* roamed over the sand between, making a direct path to it impossible.

"What can we do?" Jack asked.

"We can't stay 'ere," Tommy replied, peering through the smoke that was drifting along the channel from the wreck above them. "It's only a matter of time before they find us, and then we won't have a chance. We need to find somewhere safer to 'ide."

"There's an island." The two friends stared at Alice. She was as filthy and ragged as everyone else, but her eyes, above her tear-stained cheeks, were hard. "It's just downstream from the temple. Gordon used to take me there for picnics. It's not much but there are a few trees and some underbrush. We might be able to hide there."

"Good," Tommy said. "The breeze is blowing the smoke that way. If we keep low in the water, we might get through unnoticed"

"Our Father who art in heaven. Hallowed by Thy name." The padre's voice rose in prayer. "Thy kingdom come. Thy will be done." The fugitives gathered in closer and murmured the comforting words.

"Come on," Tommy instructed. The three slid past the end of the boat, crouched so that only their heads were above water, and moved off.

"Deliver us from evil," Jack heard as they moved away. A little later he thought he heard screams coming from behind the boat, but they could have come from somewhere else.

Jack made the journey to the island in a daze. It was as if his mind, numbed by the atrocities he had already witnessed, blocked out anything more. He staggered through the water, trying to keep as low as possible while musket balls whined above. All three were hit, but not seriously: Alice's arm was grazed, Jack received a deeper gash to his thigh and Tommy picked up a flesh wound in his right shoulder.

After what seemed like a lifetime, they pulled themselves through several mutilated bodies that had collected in a bloody eddy and crawled into the underbrush. It was not thick enough to give complete protection, but it did shield them from the mutineers who were still busy slaughtering the wounded and rummaging through the clothes of the dead.

As the three peered back out on the devastation, Jack was overcome by the scale of the horror. Every boat he could see was disabled or burning and the riverbed was covered with bodies. Of the seven hundred or so who had begun the pitiful march out of the entrenchment two hours before, Jack could only see a handful who were still standing. They were all women or young children and they were being collected in the shallows by the temple—the two blond boys were among them, still holding hands.

Everywhere else, the sand was covered with corpses. Some lay in groups behind the false shelter of a boat, but most lay alone where sword or musket had cut down their frantic attempts at escape. Every channel of the river contained its complement of floating corpses and the water was red with their blood. Here and there, men and women, some sporting hideous wounds, crawled about until put out of their misery by a *sepoy*'s musket shot or a *sowar*'s sword.

"Oh, God," Alice said, her voice breaking with emotion. "Those poor children."

"Devils!" Tommy cursed. "They had this planned all along."

"They're not killing everyone," Jack observed.

The trio watched as the *sepoys* searched along the bank of the river. Occasionally, a sword flashed, but several women and children were being pulled out of their pitiful hiding places and forced over to join the larger group by the temple.

Eventually the group, more than a hundred Jack guessed, was herded back up the ravine toward the town.

"Maybe you should surrender," Jack suggested to Alice. "It's not safe here. The killing has stopped and they are taking the women and children somewhere."

"As hostages," Alice said. "I do not envy their fate. When Havelock and the relief column do get here, do you think Nana Sahib will want to leave any witnesses to this?" She waved her hand at the view.

"Well, we can't stay 'ere," Tommy said, pulling his watch from his pocket. "It's only noon and they will be sure to search this island before long."

Jack was shocked. They had left the entrenchment at ten. All the horror should have taken longer than that. His thoughts were interrupted by the sound of firing from down river.

"Perhaps one of the boats made it away," Tommy said, looking toward the sound. "If we can work our way down river to it, and if there are enough soldiers on board, we might be able to fight our way to Allahabad yet."

Most of the *sepoys* ignored the firing and kept on with their grisly plunder, but several began to move down the river. With mounting fear, Jack noticed that a party of four, accompanied by a *sowar*, was heading in their direction.

"They're coming this way," he hissed.

"Keep down," Tommy instructed, clutching his musket. "Keep that sword ready, Jackie boy."

Almost too scared to breathe, Jack watched as the men worked their way closer. Their progress was slow because they were often sidetracked to examine a body, but they always returned toward the island.

"It's Hari," Jack said as they got close enough to be recognizable. "What's he doing with them?"

As he watched, Jack saw that Hari was taking no part in the plunder. He sat on his horse, behind the *sepoys*, occasionally exchanging words with them, but never dismounting.

"If they keep coming the way they are," Tommy whispered, "they'll fall over us. Wait until they get close. I'll give the word, then we'll charge them. The gunpowder's wet. I can't fire the musket, so I'll 'ave to use the bayonet, but the surprise'll give us an advantage. Swing the sword low, it's more difficult to parry there and if you take off a man's leg, it'll stop 'im and give you a chance to finish 'im off."

"All right," Jack murmured, feeling anything but all right.

As the *sepoys* approached, Jack tensed more and more. His hand was so tight on the sabre's hilt that he doubted he could let go even if he wanted to. He felt like throwing up. He had killed men already during the siege, but that had been impersonal, at long range. Here, if they were to survive, he would have to get close enough to someone to hack at them with a sword. The thought of metal slicing through flesh, his own or someone else's, made his stomach churn. Surely they were close enough now. Why didn't Tommy give the word?

All at once, the underbrush to Jack's left exploded. A ragged figure in civilian clothes burst out and ran. He didn't get far, one of the *sepoys* raised his musket and the man collapsed in the shallows only a few feet from the island.

"Now!" Tommy yelled, taking advantage of the distraction. He burst from cover with Jack close behind. Both screamed like maniacs as much to give themselves courage as to try and scare the enemy.

Jack had an impression of a tableau of figures staring at him in shock before Tommy was among them and his bayonet was embedded in the closest *sepoy*'s chest.

Jack concentrated on the man on the left and ran straight at him sword raised. The man lifted his musket but he was too slow. Ducking low, Jack swung the sabre with all his might. He was vaguely surprised how little resistance the man's flesh gave to the sharp blade as it sliced deep into his waist. The *sepoy* dropped his musket and began frantically trying to hold the two sides of the huge wound in his side together. It was no use. Blood gushed out and he slumped to the ground.

Jack turned to see Tommy engaged in a life and death struggle with the third *sepoy*. Both had muskets with bayonets fixed and were circling each other, looking for an opening. The fourth *sepoy* stood a bit back, his musket raised, but wavering indecisively, unable to get a clear shot.

Tommy lunged, parrying the musket aside and stabbing at the man's chest. He partly succeeded. The *sepoy*'s bayonet was pushed away from Tommy's chest, but the man dodged briskly aside and his lunge caught Tommy a slicing blow along his ribs. Working by instinct and hundreds of hours of training, Tommy swivelled his body and brought the heavy stock of his musket up under the *sepoy*'s chin. The man's head snapped back with a sickening crack and he collapsed like a limp doll.

The surviving *sepoy* aimed his musket at Tommy who stood too far from the man to use the bayonet. The *sepoy* suspected nothing before Hari's sword caught his neck, decapitating him.

Jack ran to Tommy and supported him.

"Get back in trees, please," Hari said, urging his horse forward.

When they were safely back in cover beside Alice, Hari dismounted and stood before them, placing his horse so that it blocked the small party from view.

"Thank you." It was all Jack could think of saying.

Hari nodded. "You must be hurrying. Soon others will come to be searching island. Can your friend travel?"

"I'll be all right," Tommy said through gritted teeth. "It's bleeding a lot, but it's not deep."

Again, Hari's nod. "Very well. Here." He threw down the bundle of clothes he had tried to make Jack wear the day before. "I am most sorry, but only enough for one. In any case, you are being too much white." Hari looked at Tommy.

Jack unwrapped the bundle and pulled out a *dhoti*, a loose linen jacket and a *pagri*.

"You must be remembering the words I was teaching you. What is your caste?"

"I have none," Jack replied. "I am untouchable—*mleccha*."

"That is good. You are unclean, people will be avoiding you. You will be a Lascar from Gujerat, they speak differently."

"What about Tommy and Alice?"

"You and your soldier friend must be staying in the river. Hide by day and travel by night. Beware of *muggars*—how you say, crocodiles. I will take the little memsahib with me."

"What?" As far as Jack had thought about things, he had imagined all three escaping down river. The thought of splitting up scared him.

"It must be so," Hari said. "Two can move with more ease than three. I have clothes and the little memsahib is dark like you. Many *sowars* have taken of the Eurasian girls from the entrenchment. She will not be noticed. But we must be hurrying."

Jack didn't know what to do. What Hari was saying made sense—they would all be safer under his plan—but Jack had dreamed of rescuing Alice.

"He's right," Alice said, standing up. "The most dangerous part is escaping from here. You will do better without me, and Hari will be able to take me back into town."

Alice took a step towards Hari.

"Alice!" Jack said, his voice choking.

"We must," she said turning back to look at Jack, "and we must do it now, before others come this way."

"I will find the relief column and come back for you."

"Thank you," Alice said, smiling. "But stay safe. Hari will take care of me."

Hari nodded at Jack then mounted his horse and pulled

Alice up onto the saddle in front of him. "I will be stopping anyone coming to this place, but I cannot for long. You must be taking your friend across the island. The trees will shield you from prying eyes. Find something that floats and follow the current. Good luck."

Hari pulled on the horse's reins and cantered through the shallow water past the bodies of the four *sepoys*. Jack watched him go with an aching feeling of loss. Would he ever see Hari or Alice again?

Yes! He would escape and come back. He swore he would.

Jack undressed and put on the native clothes. They made him feel strangely free.

"Are you ready to go?" he asked Tommy.

"Never more so, me old china."

"We'd better get rid of that red jacket of yours."

Tommy winced as he pulled the jacket off his shoulder. The right side of his shirt was soaked in blood.

"Let me see that."

There was a long gash running diagonally across Tommy's side. It looked nasty, but the bleeding appeared to have slowed. Jack took the old shirt he had discarded and tied it as tightly as he could around his friend's body.

"Let's hope that holds it. Let's get out of here."

Tommy reached for his musket.

"No," Jack said. "We have to leave the weapons. They will make swimming difficult and give us away if we are spotted. We'll have to rely on luck."

Reluctantly, Tommy let the musket fall. "I hope we have a lot of that."

The pair worked their way the few yards across the island and slid into the channel. It was deep enough to have a noticeable current and they relaxed and let it carry them downstream. With some of that luck Jack had mentioned, anyone looking from the shore would just see two more bodies floating down from the massacre.

By nightfall, the young men were exhausted. As the blood red sun set, they dragged themselves onto an island and found a hollow sheltered by some underbrush. Both knew they should continue under cover of darkness but neither had the strength. All day they had to stay afloat as the current swirled them down river. Whenever possible, they had held onto drifting debris, but the fickle current kept pulling them into cul-de-sacs, forcing them to fight back out into the main channel. Once they had seen a boat in the distance but had been unable to catch it and three times they had been spotted and fired upon from the shore.

"We can't go on like this." Tommy had suffered more than Jack. The water and the effort had combined to keep the bayonet wound in his side open and he had lost a lot of blood. "I don't reckon we 'ave made more than four or five miles and we were lucky to escape those times we were spotted."

"We'll rest up tomorrow and travel at night."

"That won't work neither. If we are not discovered during the day, travelling at night will be even slower. We won't know we're in a side channel until we bump into the end. It'll double the distance we 'ave to go. And what'll we do for food?"

"I'll go into a village. I know enough words to beg a bowl of rice."

"That might work but 'ow will you explain taking the bowl out into the river?"

"I'll think of something." Jack felt his old frustration at Tommy's negativity rise again.

"I already 'ave. The only way to reach the relief column is over land."

"But—"

Tommy held up a hand to stop Jack's objection. "I know what you're going to say—I wouldn't last five minutes after we were spotted—and you're right. That's why you must go alone."

"No." Jack spoke without thinking, following his instincts—what other choice was there? "I deserted Aunt Katherine and Alice. I won't desert you."

"It's not desertion. It's a sensible military decision. The only one we can make in the circumstances."

"Absolutely not. I'm not in the army. I don't have to make sensible military decisions. I will not desert you and that is final. We'll work our way a bit farther down river before dawn. That boat we saw can't be far away. We'll catch up to it and then everything will be fine."

Tommy was silent for so long in the darkness that Jack wondered if he had gone to sleep or passed out from the effects of his wound. At length he sighed. "I wish you were a soldier, then I could order you to do the sensible thing." He paused for a moment before continuing. "All right.

We'll do it your way, but first we 'ave to rest. If we sleep for a few hours, we'll still 'ave time to travel before it gets light."

"Okay," Jack agreed. "I'm sorry for what I said last night. I didn't mean it. The last few weeks have made me a bit crazy."

"They made everyone a bit crazy. At least we are still alive to be crazy, that's more than can be said for those poor devils back at Sati Chowra Ghat."

They lay in silence, remembering the scenes of horror they had witnessed. If Jack lived to be a hundred, they would never leave him. And he was going to live, he was determined about that. Maybe not to a hundred, but at least long enough to return to Cawnpore to rescue Alice.

"Dammit!" Tommy was shaking something.

"What is it?"

"My kettle. Being in the river all day. It's not working."

"You couldn't see it in the dark anyway."

"No, but I like to listen to the sound. It's relaxing. Remember your promise: if anyffing 'appens to me make sure that my watch gets back to Dad in London."

"Nothing's going to happen to you."

"Promise, if it does."

"All right, I promise."

"Thank you. Now go to sleep. That's an order."

"Yes, sir."

Jack settled as comfortably as possible on the hard ground. His mind was a whirl of memories and fears, questions and worries. He didn't want to go to sleep, scared of the dreams that would come, but exhaustion overtook him and he drifted off.

Sunday, June 28

The cool rain on Jack's face woke him. It was still dark, but the sky was already lightening to the east. They had slept too long, but the rain was good. It would swell the river and help them along once they found the boat.

Jack stretched his stiff limbs and rolled over onto something hard. Reaching under him, he felt the rounded shape of Tommy's watch. Tommy was never without his watch. It must have fallen out of his pocket in the night.

"Tommy, you dropped your watch."

There was no reply.

Jack sat up and looked around. In the grey semi-dark, there was no sign of his friend. Realization flooded over him.

"Tommy!" he said, as loudly as he dared. There was no reply.

Jack stuffed the watch into his jacket and crawled through the underbrush. Maybe Tommy had just gone to relieve himself. Even as he thought it, Jack knew it wasn't true. Tommy was gone. He had wandered off in the night to force Jack to save himself.

Jack peered out at the river. The rain hadn't yet made much difference to the water level, but it was getting heavier. As the light strengthened, he saw figures along the bank, washing themselves and their clothes in preparation for the day. Tendrils of smoke rose from cooking fires in a village on the hill above the bank. The smell of India waking up—sharp wood smoke and sweet spices—tickled his nostrils. Everything looked so calm and peaceful, it was hard to believe that the horrors of yesterday were anything but a dream. There was no sign of Tommy.

Jack lay still and thought. Tommy leaving on his own was suicide, but Jack doubted his friend would just walk into a village and give himself up. He would try to go down the river, struggling to escape as long as he could. Perhaps Jack could catch up and talk some sense into him.

With a last look at the village, Jack crossed the island, slid down the bank and pushed through the half-submerged tree roots into the chest-deep water. The rain was heavy now, hissing into the river. Jack didn't notice the soft splash behind him.

The crocodile was still young. In time, he would grow to almost thirteen feet in length and weigh more than four hundred pounds, but at five years old, he was less than half that. The eating this season had been particularly good with large amounts of meat floating downstream and snagging in the roots outside his lair in the bank. It was plentiful, but he preferred to take live food. That was why he had slipped into the water when he heard the splash. From the sound, it was something he could handle; not a buffalo, it would be many years before he could take on one of those, but perhaps a small pig or one of those two-legged creatures that lived over on the river bank. He would be able to drag it under, drown it and haul it into his den to consume at leisure. Propelled forward by the side-to-side motion of his powerful tail and with only his eyes and snout above the water, the crocodile stalked its prey.

Jack crouched down so that only his head was above water. Half swimming, half pushing off the bottom, he propelled himself with the current. The first he knew of the attack was feeling a heavy blow to his side. There was no pain, just the sensation of being shoved forcefully and a sense that something big was attached to him.

Jack survived because the crocodile miscalculated. It hit him at the wrong angle, forcing him up out of the water rather than dragging him under. It would not have made much difference to the outcome had the blow not thrust Jack back against the bank of the island and allowed him to grab onto a protruding root.

Jack held on for dear life, even when he felt the sharp teeth grate along his ribcage. The crocodile shook its head, trying to dislodge Jack, but all it succeeded in doing was tearing off half his jacket and a large strip of flesh. The blood tasted good in its mouth and the crocodile automatically jerked its head back, thrusting the flesh and material down its throat.

Jack saw the head rise from the water in a froth of blood—his blood—and torn white cloth. The head snapped back and splashed down. Frantically, Jack hauled on the branch. He had to get out of the water. If the beast got a good grip on him, he was dead. His left arm felt oddly heavy and his side ached, but he kept at it.

A quick glance showed the huge head sweeping in for a second attack. Jack screamed then and kicked wildly. He felt his foot strike something scaly and something sharp score along his leg. Then he was out of the water, frantically pulling himself through the tangle of roots.

Eventually, he reached open ground and collapsed. He tried to sit up, but he didn't have the strength. His side and his leg were beginning to hurt. He was shivering and felt feverish, and something warm was flooding over his almost useless left arm. As the adrenaline in his body dispersed, his imagination kicked in. He began to shake uncontrollably. There was to be no escape and no heroic return to rescue Alice. He was going to die, slowly and painfully, of blood loss and fever on this island. Already his sight was dimming as he slipped toward oblivion. The last thing Jack saw through the haze that was enveloping his vision was a blurred pair of naked, muddy feet. Then he passed out.

PART V

The Return

Thursday, July 16

The colour of his skin saved Jack's life. The boys who were out collecting wood on the island and discovered his body assumed he was from a neighbouring village. They also assumed he was going to die. They had seen enough crocodile wounds to know a bad one when they saw it. The whole left side of Jack's chest had been ripped open and a large flap of skin removed. The calf and thigh of his left leg was also badly cut and his entire body was covered in blood. Nevertheless, the boys ran back to their village and told what they had found. Four men came, bound Jack's wounds as best they could and carried his limp body home. There, because he was still young, the women took over, shooing the men away and installing him in a dark recess at the back of a hut.

For eleven days Jack hovered between life and death. At times his fever rose to dangerous levels and he twisted and turned, babbling incoherently. At others he lay like a corpse, his breathing noticeable only by the misting of the polished tin plate one of the women held under his nose. Through it all, the women bathed his wounds, fed him as much milk as they could force down and prayed to

Dhanwantri, doctor to the gods, for his recovery. For one of those reasons, or perhaps because of all three, on day twelve Jack opened his eyes.

Over the next eight days, Jack gradually regained a little strength. He began to eat fruit, lentils, rice and chapattis. The gashes in his leg were not deep and healed well. His chest recovered too, although more slowly and he could not use his left arm for fear of opening the wound. Because of this, the mass of scar tissue that filled in the hollow where the crocodile had eaten a part of him formed tightly and, for the rest of his life, he could not raise that arm higher than his shoulder.

To begin with, Jack kept silent and feigned dumbness, not wanting to betray his real heritage. It was unnecessary. He had talked deliriously in English and the women had kept silent whenever *sepoys* wandered through the village.

As time passed, rumours arrived of the approach of an avenging army of *feringhee* warriors. Eventually, the sound of cannon fire could be heard from the Grand Trunk Road. This persuaded Jack, over the pleading of the women, to leave the village. He was only a few miles from Cawnpore and he had to try to find Alice.

The women dressed him in fresh clothes, a *dhoti* and *pagri*, and wrapped his still painful chest in cloth. The men of the village gave him a long staff to help him walk. With a rice bowl over his shoulder, Jack looked like one of he thousands of itinerant beggars who were scattered across the country in the wake of the mutiny's chaos. Slowly, and feeling as if his legs were made of water, he limped toward Cawnpore.

Where Soldiers Lie

At first, Jack was scared that someone would challenge him, but as he progressed and was ignored, his confidence grew. One more crippled beggar excited no one's interest. Besides, everyone had more important things to worry about. The sound of cannons was coming inexorably closer and the flood of *sepoys* fleeing north was getting stronger all the time. It was obvious that Nana Sahib was losing the battle to preserve his new kingdom.

The going was slow and Jack had to stop often to rest but by late afternoon, he could see the blackened ruins of the entrenchment ahead of him. It was the only place he could think of to begin his search.

As Tommy had predicted, the rains had all but washed away the mud wall behind which the defenders had huddled for so many days. All that was left was a low mound and a line of puddles where the trench had been. The blackened, skeletal ruins of the two roofless barrack buildings stood as a grim reminder of the unimaginable suffering they had contained. Graffiti defaced the walls. Some were pitiful pleas—"God help us!"—others were lists of the dead, "Little George, 8th June; Lilly, 12th June; Aunt May, 13th June; Mother, 18th June."

All around, the cannon-scarred ground was covered with soggy scraps of paper and cloth, fragments of furniture, tattered shoes and broken glass. A flock of obscenely fat vultures squabbled around the sepulchral well, pigs rooted in the ground, and scattered human bones poked whitely out of the brown mud Over everything hung the damp smell of decay and rot.

Jack stumbled through the ruins, tears springing to his eyes as he recognized places that had meant so much: the place where he had found Australian, the doorway where Charles Hillersdon had been disemboweled, the hospital room from which he had dragged the soldier with the useless legs.

Gradually, Jack worked his sad way to the room where the Wheelers had lived. Gordon's blood was still visible, a dark stain on one wall. Jack shuffled over to the corner where Lady Wheeler and Alice usually sat. Jack didn't know what to look for, but he couldn't think of anywhere else to go. The room was just as desolate and empty as the rest of the building. This had been a stupid idea. He couldn't ask anyone where the memsahib was and he didn't have the strength to wander around the town on what would probably be a futile search. He slumped down against the wall.

On the opposite wall, someone had scratched a single word—Bibighar. Jack gazed at the black letters for a moment. His first meeting with Alice seemed like a million years ago—a different world. Now she was lost. Jack's eyes misted over and he raised his arm to wipe the tears that were beginning to form. Then he stopped. Bibighar! The letters were darker, fresher, than the rest of the writing. With a violent jerk that sent arrows of pain lancing through his side, Jack stood up. What did it mean? Was it a message? It had to be. Leaning heavily on his stick, Jack struggled out of the barracks, splashed across the remains of the trench and into the ruins of the town.

All around him was destruction, shattered trees, blackened bungalows, and destroyed carts and furniture.

Animals roamed at will through the streets and vultures squabbled over scattered remains. Terrified townspeople and downcast *sepoys* flowed past Jack, ignoring him completely. A few words reached him from the babble of the throng—battle, defeat, flight, revenge. Ignoring it all, Jack plodded slowly on, past St. John's Church, the native infantry lines, the blackened skeleton of Aunt Katherine's bungalow and the remains of General Wheeler's house.

As he approached the gardens surrounding the Bibighar, Jack noticed a strange thing: it was becoming oddly quiet. There were no animals or birds around to make noise and even the fleeing people seemed to be avoiding the area, sweeping around it like a stream around a rock. And there was a hideous, sickly sweet smell, which got stronger as he advanced.

Ignoring the pain in his body, Jack moved as fast as he could, fighting back the nausea that the smell and his sense of foreboding were creating. At last he reached the gate in the low wall where he had sat to imagine the poor, hanged *bibi*.

The wooden door in the centre of the Bibighar was closed. As Jack stumbled forward the smell became almost unbearable and a peculiar droning noise began. On the threshold, Jack stopped, his need to look in balanced by his desire to leave. But he had to know. He forced himself forward and leaned on the door. It gave inward with a harsh shriek of rusted hinges. A dense, black cloud of fat flies, the source of the droning, took to the air, forcing Jack to close his eyes and cover his face with his good arm. Although the smell made him gag, he took a tentative step forward, his bare foot strangely sticky as he raised it from the ground. Finally, he dropped his arm and opened his eyes. For the rest of his life, he wished he had kept them closed.

The doorway led directly into the inner courtyard where the mulsoori tree stood. The courtyard measured sixteen by forty feet and the ground was completely covered with a thick layer of congealing blood—the sticky substance underfoot, Jack realized. Torn papers, books, fragments of clothing, ladies' bonnets, children's shoes and tresses of hair lay bright against the dark floor. The courtyard walls were splashed with blood, as if it had been thrown from a bucket. Here and there bloody hand prints were smeared, the smallest closest to the ground. The mulsoori tree was decorated with fragments of cloth and its branches and trunk glistened wetly. It is weeping blood, Jack thought.

Jack felt his stomach rise and turned to collapse retching on the ground. What horror had happened here? How many women and children had died to produce so much blood? Was Alice's blood on that floor?

Jack dragged himself to his feet and, using the wall for support, lurched around the building. At the corner he stopped. Forty feet away, across the trampled grass, stood the sprawling banyan tree and, under it, the old stone well. A path of blood led from the Bibighar to the well as if something heavy, or many things, had been dragged there. Not certain how much more he could take, Jack tottered forward.

"You would be most advised not to be looking down there, Jack Sahib. I have seen and I pray to all the gods that

I die before I behold such a sight again."

Jack looked up to see Hari's familiar figure standing beside the compound wall. He no longer wore the uniform of a *sowar* and was dressed as he used to be, as Aunt Katherine's stable boy.

"What has happened, Hari?" Jack asked, weakly.

"There has been a most terrible evil in this place," Hari replied.

"Alice?" Jack found it difficult to say her name.

"The little memsahib lives."

Relief flooded over Jack. The tensions of the day, the uncertainty of not knowing Alice's fate and the horrors of the courtyard melted away. With them went the last of Jack's strength and he slumped to the ground.

"Come, young sahib." Hari helped Jack to his feet. "It is not far and the memsahib is being most eager to see you."

Leaning heavily on Hari, Jack stumbled along. Their journey was a blur of noise and moving figures. All Jack could think was that he was going to see Alice again.

Eventually, the pair arrived at a sweetmeat shop in the twisted alleys of the native city. Hari walked in and nodded to the owner. He said something in rapid Hindi and ushered Jack through a curtain into a back room.

For an instant, Jack wondered why Hari had brought him to this place. A high-caste Indian girl sat on a pile of embroidered cushions. She wore a brightly coloured *sari* and the single red *tika* mark of a married woman on her forehead. Her hands were elaborately patterned with lines of brown henna. She looked up as Jack entered and leaped to her feet.

"Jack!" Alice exclaimed, and then she was embracing him. He winced at the pressure on his side.

Alice drew back. "You're wounded?"

Jack nodded weakly.

"Come and sit." Alice and Hari helped Jack onto the cushions and arranged them so that he was comfortable.

"I will get tea," Hari announced and disappeared through the curtain.

"You're alive," Jack said.

"Yes and by the looks of things I have fared better than you. Tell me your story."

Briefly, Jack related what he could remember of his ordeal. He cried when he told her about Tommy.

"At least you have his watch," Alice said.

"No. The crocodile ate that along with most of my jacket and a piece of my side. But what happened to you?"

Alice's face became troubled as she recalled the massacre. "I'll never know how we made it through. Wounded men, women and children were being butchered everywhere around us, but Hari just rode straight on. We were challenged several times but Hari talked his way out of it. I think he said he had stolen me for a wife and made some vulgar joke that everyone laughed at.

"Anyway, he took me to some women who dressed me like this. Then we came here. I think I was in shock. I just remember doing whatever Hari or the women told me, without question. It all seemed unreal somehow. It was only a day or two later that it sank in. Mother, father, all those hundreds of innocent, helpless people killed. It was almost more than I could bear. When Hari told me that about two hundred women and children had been taken to the Bibighar, I wanted desperately to go and join them. I think I thought that by joining them, I would somehow be going back to before this all began."

"I'm glad you didn't. I've just been there."

"Hari told me what happened there." Alice's eye filled with tears. "It was only yesterday. We thought it was going to be all right, since there was fighting just a few miles down the road.

"But they went in with swords and slaughtered everyone—Rose Greenaway, the survivors from the river, all those children. Then, this morning, they went back and threw the bodies down the well by the banyan tree. They had to chop them up to make them fit. Hari said some of the children were still alive."

Alice covered her face with her hands and broke into heaving sobs. Jack put his good arm around her shoulder.

After a few moments she looked up at Jack and smiled weakly through her tears. "You're always there to comfort me."

"I hope so," Jack said.

Alice's smile faded. "Is this ever going to end?"

"Soon, I think. Havelock and Neill are at the edge of town. There has been a big battle and it looks like the *sepoys* are defeated. The soldiers will be here tomorrow."

"That won't end it."

"But with the mutineers defeated—"

"What do you think Havelock's highlanders will do once they hear what happened at Sati Chowra Ghat and look down the well at the Bibighar?"

Alice answered her own question. "They will go berserk. No one with a black skin will be safe. I have heard what they've done in other places with much less provocation. Drunk on rum, they defile Hindus by forcing them to eat beef and Muslims by stuffing pork down their throats. They decorate trees with hanged bodies and blow prisoners from the mouths of cannons. I, for one, want no part of it."

"What do you mean?"

Alice looked Jack in the eye for a long moment. "I mean that I don't want to go back." Before Jack could say anything, she went on. "I have done a lot of thinking in this room. There is nothing for me to go back to. My family is dead and, after the pity has worn off, I will be just another half-caste.

"Oh, I am sure because I am the heroic general's daughter—the only survivor of the horrors of Cawnpore—I will be allowed some position in society. If nothing else, I will be invited places as a curiosity. But, however well I seem to do, there will always be voices whispering behind my back. And if I dare to speak my mind, I will be dismissed as a hysterical women, deranged by the terrible experience she suffered. It would be a horrible sham of a life that would drive me to the insane asylum at Bedlam more surely than anything I have lived through here."

"But you cannot live among the natives!"

"Why not? Would it not be proper? I am close enough in colour to fit in. I am learning how to behave and," Alice spread the folds of the sari about her, "I like the clothes."

"But . . . " Jack was desolate. He had driven himself to

find Alice because he had some half-formed idea that, when this was all over, they would be together in a perfect world. Now it seemed that he had found her only to lose her again. His mind was a jumble of questions. "What will you do? How will you live? Where will you get money?"

"It is cheap to live here if your expectations are not too high. And I have some money. Before we fled to the entrenchment, father had a strongbox of rupees buried beneath the bungalow. Hari has checked and the spot is undisturbed. It is not a king's ransom, but I will be able to get by quite nicely for a long time."

"But the mutineers tried to kill us all."

"Yes, but they were soldiers led by a despot. Most Indians kept low and waited. And many helped—the women who dressed me and healed you. There are as many good and bad people here as anywhere else."

"I suppose so, but what will you do?"

"I will study. I will read the ancient books and stories; they have always fascinated me. Perhaps I will even translate some. I don't know if this is all I will do forever. But for now, I don't think I want to return to the brutal world we have lived in." She paused for a moment, playing with the embroidered hem of her *sari*. "Will you join me?"

It took Jack a moment to realize what Alice was asking. "Wh . . . What?" he stammered.

Alice laughed. "You look so stunned. But why not? You said that *your* dream was to find a lost city. Is this not the perfect opportunity? I will read the texts and tell you where to look and you can go and find them."

"It sounds so easy."

"It won't be. But at least we will be doing what we want to do, not what everyone else wants."

Jack thought for a long time. With Tommy lost and his aunt and uncle dead, there was nothing to pull him back to proper society, and the idea of finally being able to go out on his own and do what *he* wanted was immensely attractive. Not to mention being able to do these things with Alice. The last few weeks in Cawnpore had given him a different perspective—the experience of living with sudden, random death, of being grateful to be alive at the end to eat a handful of lentils and a cupful of tepid water would make it difficult to take a society tea party seriously. But it was still a frightening risk. He'd be cutting himself loose from all that he knew, allowing himself to be absorbed into a foreign culture. Could he do it?

Jack was distracted by Hari's return. He was carrying a silver tray loaded with china cups and a blue and white teapot.

"Would anyone be wishing for a most refreshing cup of tea?"

Jack burst out laughing. "Yes, Hari. I would love a nice cup of tea."

As Hari poured, Jack asked him, "What will you do now, Hari?"

"I am thinking I will be going for a short walk in the mountains. It is, I am told, where the gods live." Hari nodded his head enigmatically. "And you, Jack Sahib? What is it you will be doing?"

Jack looked at Alice and smiled. "I am going to discover a lost city."

Epilogue

Sunday, June 27, 1897

Jack struggled up from the depths of his memory well. Life had gone on while he had been remembering. The pelicans and kingfishers were still busily feeding, but the laundresses had finished and were returning to shore with their bundles. The British officer—a general Jack noted from the splendid uniform—was now close by. Lightly, Jack jumped to his feet as the officer approached. Dressed in loose Indian clothes, Jack was indistinguishable from the dozens of other people on the banks of the river.

"Sahib, I would talk with you," he said in flawless Hindi.

The officer ignored him.

"Sahib," Jack tried again. "Will you not talk with a loyal subject of the Little Queen on her most auspicious jubilee?"

The officer barely glanced Jack's way.

"So, now that you're a mighty general," Jack shouted after him in English, "you won't talk to your old china plate."

The soldier reigned in his horse and turned to stare hard at Jack.

"You've done well for a fishmonger's son." Jack could keep a straight face no longer.

"Jack?" the general asked.

"None other," Jack said through his laughter. "And, if I am not much mistaken, you are General Thomas Mallory Davies, son of the best fishmonger in Whitechapel."

Tommy dismounted and stepped forward. "I thought you were dead."

"I thought the same of you."

The pair embraced. They were both old men now, but in a single moment the years fell away and it was the summer of 1857 again.

"How did you find me?" Tommy stared at Jack with a puzzled look on his face.

"I read the *India Gazette*. They made quite a fuss of you coming to take over the garrison here. But come, let's sit on the steps. We have some stories to tell, I think."

Tommy tethered his horse and sat beside his old friend. "You look like a native."

"And you look like a general." They both laughed.

"You go first," Jack said. "How did you survive the river?"

"After I left you, I was sure I was going to die. That was why I left my watch. Do you still have it?"

"I'm afraid not. It is in the belly of a crocodile."

"I loved that watch," Tommy said, regretfully. "Anyway, I thought I would go down river as long as I had strength. As it turned out, the boat that escaped from here was stuck on a sandbar just around the corner. I wanted to come back and get you, but they were in a hurry to be off before we attracted too much attention from the shore.

"We went some few miles farther on the river before

the boat became completely stuck. A large party of villagers and *sepoys* was advancing. It looked like the end. About fifteen of us decided that it would be better to die fighting in an attempt to give the boat time to get off.

"We charged the crowd. It was a wild melee, I can tell you. Several of us holed up in a small temple and kept the rabble at bay for some hours. Eventually, they set fire around us and we had to break for the river. Most didn't make it, but five of us did. There was no sign of the boat, so we swam for it, musket balls splashing all around.

"I don't know how we managed, but we got downstream and dragged ourselves out, more dead than alive. We didn't care what happened but, by some miracle, we picked a village that had remained loyal. The local Rajah, Dirigibijah Singh, was a cantankerous old savage, but he had stayed loyal just to annoy his neighbour who supported the rebels. We stayed with him for weeks until the relief column pacified the country around us.

"By then, Havelock had taken Cawnpore back but was having the devil's own job at Lucknow. He got there in September but with too few men to break out, so he was besieged with the defenders. I went up with Sir Colin Campbell and put the matter right in November.

"I was back in Cawnpore in December for the final battle there and was lucky enough to capture a cannon. They breveted me captain for that. I searched everywhere, hoping that you or Alice had been in hiding all those months, but I could find no sign. I assumed you had both been killed. Since then it has been soldiering and fighting in all kinds of godforsaken spots. It is possible to rise in this man's army without money and powerful friends, but it is a lot of hard work."

"And on your way, you have lost your accent."

"Gawd, so I 'ave."

The pair laughed.

"But what happened to you?"

"I was set to follow you downriver, but a crocodile had other ideas. He took your watch and a piece of me."

"May they both give him indigestion."

"Luckily, I was found by some villagers who cared for me. When I had healed a little, I came back here looking for Alice."

"Did you find her?"

"I did, and Hari too."

"Then why did you not come back?"

"Alice wasn't going to, so I decided to stay with her. I wanted more freedom than I could have had after the mutiny, when things had gone back to the same as before. And it has worked. We had a little money and we have made some more. Alice translates old texts—under a false name, of course—and I have done odds and ends that have cropped up."

"Did you ever find your lost city?"

"I did. It was where Alice said in would be, under a hill in the Indus valley."

"But I've never heard of it!"

"To do more than the minor scratchings that I have done would require a government expedition, and I would either have to step aside and be anonymous or come back into the culture I've left. I didn't want either. And besides, perhaps lost cities are best left lost. Although, I daresay someone will find it one day. When they do, it will turn all our ideas about this country on their heads."

Tommy nodded. "We have all done well enough. But what of Hari?"

"Last I heard, he was still alive, tramping around the mysterious places on the edge of the Empire, counting his steps as he goes."

The pair sat in companionable silence as the huge sun sank swiftly below the horizon.

"I've never been able to get used to that," Jack commented.

"Me neither," said Tommy. He pulled a fancy gold watch out of his pocket and checked the time. "I must be off. There's a dinner to celebrate the Queen's Jubilee in the mess tonight. The mighty general should be there at the head of the table."

Tommy and Jack rose and stretched. Tommy hauled himself into the saddle and turned his horse toward the ravine.

"It's turned out all right, hasn't it?" he said.

"It has," Jack agreed.

Tommy looked up at the black shapes of the vultures gathering to roost in the trees along the top of the bank. "Still and all, though. I do 'ate those birds."

Historical Note

The broad backdrop of the Indian Mutiny is accurate, as, sadly, are the horrors of Sati Chowra Ghat and the Bibighar. There were mysterious chapattis and greased cartridges, but the causes of what in India is known as the First War for Independence were immensely complex. Atrocities were committed by both sides as the tides of the war ebbed and flowed along the Ganges plain, but there were also many acts of incredible courage and humanity. After peace returned in 1858, India ceased to be the sole preserve of the East India Company and was ruled directly for almost one hundred years by the British government.

Some characters—Captain Moore, Lieutenant Boulton, General Wheeler and his son Gordon—are historical, although a few liberties have been taken with their actions. Most of these are minor, such as putting words in Captain Moore's mouth prior to the raids he led; but I have placed General Wheeler's death at Sati Chowra Ghat rather than back in Cawnpore where he was probably taken after being captured from the boat that attempted to escape downstream. Other characters—principally Jack, Tommy and Hari—are wholly fictitious, although their actions and circumstances are plausible.

Alice Wheeler is an amalgam of the old general's two daughters, Eliza and Margaret. Both supposedly survived the massacre at the river, although Eliza was probably killed at the Bibighar. It was said that some of Havelock's highlanders carried locks of her hair to keep their anger on the boil during the vengeful slaughter that followed the mutiny. Margaret was variously said to have killed herself, died of malaria or lived a peaceful life with the *sowar* who rescued her. More than fifty years after the mutiny, a missionary doctor was summoned to the deathbed of a woman in the native city of Cawnpore. The woman, speaking cultured English, stated that she was General and Lady Wheeler's youngest daughter.

The lost city that Alice read about in the Vedas and Jack searched for is Mohenjo-daro ("the place of the dead"), which was finally discovered and excavated in the 1920s. The city, and its companion, Harappa, were the first evidence of an ancient Indus Valley civilization that dates back almost five thousand years.

Four soldiers, two officers and two privates, did survive from the boat that managed to get away from Sati Chowra Ghat and were protected by Rajah Dirigibijah Singh. Of them, Gunner Sullivan died soon after of cholera; Private Murphy led tours around mutiny sites in Cawnpore and died a drunk; Lieutenant Delafosse stayed in the army, living until 1905; and Lieutenant Thomson wrote a best-selling book about his exploits and died a general in 1917.

Little from the time of the mutiny remains for the visitor to see in Cawnpore, or Kanpur as it is now known. The entrenchment is long gone, although its outline is partially marked in painted stones and All Souls Cathedral still stands. The Hardeo Temple remains, overlooking the river at Sati Chowra Ghat. The monument over the Bibighar well was dismantled after Indian Independence in 1947, leaving only a sandstone circle to mark the horrors beneath, and few visitors to the park realize what they walk on. However, some people claim the tragic site is haunted. One woman, more than a hundred years after the tragedy, noticed her dogs behaving oddly near the site of the Bibighar and looked up to see "two blond boys running this way and that around the mouth of the well . . . desperately trying to find somewhere to escape."

Finally, my father was born in 1905 in Lucknow, near the ruins of the Residency that was successfully defended against the mutineers in 1857. He lived most of his life in India, working as a civil engineer on the railways. In the late 1920s, he and a colleague went hunting and shot a crocodile by the Ganges, downstream from Cawnpore. In its stomach, they found a pocket watch engraved to a young subaltern on his departure for India in January 1857.